1500 BLAC

JOKES THAT WILL MAKE

YOUR MOTHER CRY

CLOWN DOWN

About the Author

About the Clown Down: A Tragedy Dressed in Laughter

The Down Clown isn't just a name, it's a declaration of war against the cheap sensibility and hypocrisy of the modern world. Raised in an emotional dump and fed on the crumbs of human despair, this unscrupulous narrator has dedicated his life to laughing at what others cry about. He's the bastard who will crash your funeral, not to console the mourners, but to tell you how the dead man managed to screw up even on his last day.

With a humor so black it would make a coal mine look like Disneyland, Down the Clown writes from the shadows of morality, where only the brave or the stupid dare to tread. His philosophy is simple: if you can't laugh at everything, especially the worst, then you haven't understood anything about life. His cruelty isn't gratuitous; it's a reminder that the world is a fucked up place, and the only way to survive is to laugh at it.

No one knows his real name, because if they did they would probably lynch him. But he doesn't hide. His work is an open act of emotional terrorism, and if you're offended, he invites you to send him a letter. He promises not to read it, but he'll wipe his ass with it while he writes his next book.

Copyright

Warning: This Book Is Not For Everyone

Are you sensitive? Do you have unwavering values? Do you believe in happy endings and that everyone deserves respect? Then I have bad news for you: this book is NOT for you.

"The Protagonist, Narrator, Clown Down" is a collection of dark humor jokes so crude, cruel, and vast that they could offend a stone. There are no safe zones here, no mercy, and definitely no "sorry" button. If you enter, you do so at your own risk, with the full awareness that what you find may hurt your feelings, your morals, and perhaps even your faith in humanity.

This book is designed for those who are not afraid of anything, who know how to laugh at the unthinkable, and who understand that dark humor is not for everyone, but it is definitely for the most daring. If you are one of those who get indignant easily, close this book right now and go back to your padded corner of beautiful words and inspiring phrases.

But if you decide to stay, do so knowing that you will find no limits here. The Down Clown does not respect anyone or anything, and he will not ask your permission to make you feel uncomfortable.**If you dare to cross this line, it is at your own risk. We do not give money back or sell balms for wounded souls.**

Still here? Great. Then welcome to the worst that humanity has to offer... and get ready to laugh about it.**Don't say we didn't warn you.**

CLOWN DOWN

Index

Warning
Are you brave enough to read on?

About the Author
Meet Down the Clown: A master of chaos and irreverence.

- Acid fragments of irreverent philosophy.

Conclusion: The Last Laugh

A farewell as cruel as the rest of the book.

Bonus

- *Want more? A few extra laughs courtesy of Clown Down.*

Classic Black Humor: 250 Jokes

1. What does a family do after a car accident?
   Wash your car and look for a deal on coffins.

2. What is the most fun part of a funeral?
   Nobody complains about sandwiches.

3. My grandfather died of a heart attack while playing hide and seek.
   We've been looking for it for years.

4. What do a surgeon and a butcher have in common?
   If you make a mistake, no one can blame you.

5. Why is the cemetery so popular?
   Because people are dying to get in.

6. I sold my wheelchair the other day.
   I still can't believe how the buyer got up and walked away!

7. My ex said I would never find someone like her.
   Thank God.

8. What do you call a blind man with a rifle?
   Scary.

9. My neighbor jumped off a bridge yesterday.
   At least he left his car well parked.

10. What's worse than finding a worm in your apple?
    Finding half a worm... and realizing the other half is your brother.

Here are more dark doses for you:

11. If I got paid to make a fool of myself, I'd already be starving to death.
12. My dog died yesterday.
    At least I won't have to share pizza anymore.
13. What does a disabled bird do?
    Learning to walk.

14. What do you call a sad clown?
    A good reflection of your life.
15. Why can't you joke about death?
    Because it's always the darkest punchline.
16. What's darker than a black humor joke?
    My childhood.

17. What is the best thing about cremations?
    Nobody complains that it's too hot.

18. How do you know your funeral will be boring?
    When you are the center of attention.

19. Why do orphans hate puzzles?
    Because they never find the "mom" and "dad" pieces.

20. What did the parachute say to the rookie?
    "Relax, this will be your last fall."

21. What happens if a suicide survives?
    He becomes the best comedian in his support group.

22. What do you call a Paralympic swimmer who comes in last?
    Miracle... because he jumped in without knowing how to swim!

23. What did the coffin say to the corpse?
    "Always together until the end!"

24. My girlfriend left me for being too cold.
    So I froze his bank account.

25. What is an arsonist doing in an orphanage?
    Call the place "home."

26. My ex told me that he would never forget what I did to him.
    Of course, because he still has the scar.

More Dark Delights

27. If I had a penny for every mistake I've made...

I could buy a decent funeral for everyone.

28. What do clowns and politicians have in common?
    They both make a living entertaining idiots.

29. Why do diabetics hate sweet jokes?
    Because they literally kill them.

30. What do orphans do when they have nightmares?
    Nothing. There's no one to wake them up.

31. If heaven is real, it must be full of people asking:
    "Why you and not me?"

32. I was offered a job at a funeral home.
    They said there is always room to grow.

33. What is sadder than losing a loved one?
    Discovering that he left debts.

34. What is a skeleton doing in the closet?
    He plans his triumphant exit.

35. What did the newly dug grave say?
    "This way, buddy. There's always room for one more."

36. Why can't karma be trusted?
    Because it always comes when you're already in the coffin.

Even more dark laughter

37. What happens if a surgeon has a bad day?
    Someone else remembers it... forever.

38. What's worse than losing your phone?
    Losing it during a wake... and finding it in the coffin!

39. My grandmother always said:
    "Follow your dreams!"
    Too bad he died in his sleep.

40. How does the life of a chronic insomniac end?
    With an eternal nap.

41. Why don't zombies seek psychological help?
    Because they don't have a head for such things.

42. My cousin told me:
    "You could win the lottery!"
    Yes, of course, with the same probability as surviving this book.

43. What does a vampire do when he's not hungry?
    Cavities are taken care of.

44. What's scarier than a slow death?
    A quick wedding.

45. Why do ghosts hate the living?
    Because we continue to take up space that we don't need.

46. My friend said:
    "There is nothing darker than black humor."
    I replied, "Your future."

47. What does an airplane and an unhappy marriage have in common?
    Both end in disaster if there is no emergency exit.

48. Why are clowns better than politicians?
    Because when they kill someone, at least they apologize.

49. What's the worst thing about being hit by an ice cream truck?
    That your death will be sweet, but not cold.

50. Why don't firefighters put out the fire in hell?
    Because insurance doesn't cover sinners.

51. My cousin had a prepaid cremation.
    I told him, "You're the only one who plans to die hot."

52. What did the guillotine say to the king?
    "I'll make you bow your head for the first time."

53. Why was the violinist playing at the funeral?
    Because I didn't know how to say "I'm sorry" in words.

54. My friend survived a lightning strike.
    I told him he should try his luck in the lottery... right in the storm.

55. What's worse than losing an arm?
    Find it in the soup.

56. What does a child in an orphanage do on Father's Day?
    Nothing, except to remember that it is on sale.

More dark jokes to enlighten black souls

57. If tears could bring back life,
    cemeteries would be swimming pools.

58. Why do angels hate airplane pilots?
    Because they compete for the same sky.

59. My wife said she would always support me when I fell.
    That's why he pushed the ladder.

60. What's worse than not being able to pay your mortgage?
    Finding out you live in the house you haunted.

61. My cousin jumped off a building.
    The news reported: "A shocking landing."

62. What is a dead body doing in the sea?
    Practice eternal floating.

63. What's lonelier than a ghost?
    A spirit with a limited data plan.

64. Why don't skeletons use umbrellas?
    Because they never mind getting their bones wet.

65. If the dead could speak,
    They would not stop demanding the wilted flowers that we gave them.

66. What did karma say to the murderer?
    "Don't worry, we'll see each other soon."

Delving into the dark side

67. What is a zombie doing in a brain store?
    Complain about high prices.

68. What did my alcoholic uncle say when he died?
    "I'm finally sober."

69. Why don't psychologists go to hell?
    Because they don't know how to handle more conflicting souls.

70. What's worse than forgetting a friend?
    Remember him at his own funeral.

71. What do coffins do on Black Friday?
    Offer a one-way trip at a discount.

72. If the dead lived,
    offices would be full of zombies asking for accrued vacation time.

73. Why didn't the ghost go to the gym?
    Because it was already in the form of... vapor.

74. What does a lost soul do?
    Wondering why Google Maps never loaded.

75. What did the doctor say to the terminally ill patient?
    "Get ready for a low oxygen diet."

76. My grandfather quit smoking.
    Too bad it was because we buried him.

77. What is a blind man doing with a gun in a gunfight?
    Raising the stakes.

78. My mother-in-law said she would die before she apologized.
    It seems he kept his word.

79. What did the coffin say when it was closed?
"Finally, some privacy!"

80. Why does the orphanage organize raffles?
So that children feel what it is like to be chosen.

81. What does a firefighter do at a big fire?
Practice for when I go to hell.

82. My neighbor was so lonely that even his ghosts left him.

83. Why are clowns bad drivers?
Because they are always busy laughing their heads off.

84. What's worse than dying in a traffic accident?
Be the co-pilot who said, "Accelerate!"

85. My wife said she would like to die before me.
I told her I can help her with that.

86. What's a vegan doing in heaven?
Wondering if clouds are cruelty-free.

87. Why do orphans hate family trees?
Because they never have branches.

88. What did the skull say to its grave?
"You always have me covered!"

89. What do a coffin and a wedding have in common?
Both lock someone up forever.

90. Why don't doctors joke in surgery?
Because his mistakes are already funny enough.

91. If zombies had a union,
would be demanding fresher brains.

92. What is a suicidal person doing on a diving board?
A dramatic statement.

93. What's scarier than a clown?
A clown in a coffin.

94. Why does no one want to pray for the devil?
    Because even he knows he's lost.

95. What does an amputee say to the surgeon?
    "Don't spoil my mood!"

96. What's the worst thing that can happen at a funeral?
    Let the dead man rise and criticize the decoration.

97. What does an arsonist do when he feels lost?
    Looking for a "new home" to ignite your passion.

98. My grandfather said he was afraid of fires.
    Too bad he chose to be cremated.

99. What does a vegetarian vampire do?
    Sucking tomato blood.

100. What's worse than losing the love of your life?
     Finding out that he never loved you.

Continuation up to 150

101. What does a lawyer do in hell?
     Explain that his contract did not include llamas.

102. What did the cemetery say to the sun?
     "Leave me alone, I'm already dry!"

103. What's worse than dying alone?
     Dying surrounded by people who were waiting for your inheritance.

104. Why don't ghosts scare the poor?
     Because they have nothing left to lose.

105. What does a serial killer do when he's bored?
     We move on to crossword puzzles.

106. My friend said he was tired of living.
     So I sent him on a journey of no return.

107. What did the scream say to the silence?
"I'm going to bury you in noise!"

108. What's worse than being fired?
Be hired as a medical practice corpsman.

109. Why do psychologists never get depressed?
Because they always have worse clients.

110. What's more ironic than an arsonist in the rain?
A drowning lifeguard.

111. What does a child do in a charity hospital?
Expect the doctor not to charge.

112. What does a suicidal pilot do on his day off?
Plan it.

113. What did the guillotine say to the executioner?
"You're sharp today, buddy!"

114. Why don't ghosts vote?
Because they are tired of empty promises.

115. My friend said he wanted to "go out with a bang."
So I pushed him into the ocean.

116. What's worse than losing a leg?
Let the dog take it as a toy.

117. Why does karma always arrive late?
Because he enjoys seeing you suffer a little more.

118. What is a corpse doing at a wedding?
Watching from the cake.

119. Why are funerals more expensive than weddings?
Because at least the dead don't get divorced.

120. What does a blind man do with a knife?
Cutting the voltage... accidentally.

121. What is the best thing about euthanasia?

That you don't have to pay taxes afterwards.

122.Why do coffins never have mirrors?
Because nobody wants to see how it turned out.

123.What does an orphan do when he wins a video game?
He looks for someone to dedicate his victory to... but he can't find anyone.

124.Why don't funeral homes have "buy one, get one free" deals?
Because it would be suspicious.

125.What did the hanged man say to the rope?
"Thank you for your support."

126.What do children in an orphanage do when they are afraid?
Nothing, because there is no one to call.

127.How do you know a psychopath loves you?
Because he hasn't added you to his list... yet.

128.What's faster than a divorce?
A cardiac arrest during the process.

129.What does a brainless zombie do?
Join the government.

130.What's more ironic than a suicide failing?
A firefighter getting burned on his day off.

131.What did the dead man say to the living?
"How's the wifi up there?"

132.My friend wanted to go skydiving, but he was scared.
I told him: "Don't worry, the fear goes away... just before the blow."

133.Why are weddings like funerals?
Because in both you bury your happiness.

134.My friend said that life is like a joke.
I just hope mine has a good punchline.

135. What did the dog say to the vet?

"Do it quickly, I want to go running to heaven!"

136. Why are clowns good at hiding?

Because no one is looking for them, they are busy running away from them.

137. What's sadder than a child crying at Christmas?

A child crying at Christmas... in an orphanage.

138. What does an arsonist do at a campfire?

Planning your next masterpiece.

139. What's more awkward than a bad joke?

A minute of silence later.

140. My grandfather told me that his last wish was to fly.

So we cremated it and scattered it to the wind.

Intensifying the dark side (141-250)

141. Why is the cemetery always full?

Because it's the only place where appointments never get cancelled.

142. What did the man sentenced to death say before the injection?

"I hope they at least have soft hands."

143. What did the empty tomb say to the new corpse?

"Welcome to the neighborhood!"

144. What does a suicidal person do with a stopwatch?

Measure the time you have left.

145. What's darker than black humor?

My bank account.

146. What is a ghost doing at a wedding?

Laugh at the "until death do us part" part.

147. What's worse than a bad medical diagnosis?

A good diagnosis... after your burial.

148. Why don't the dead celebrate New Year's?
Because they don't care about time anymore.

149. My neighbor died yesterday.
Now I can use your wifi.

150. What did the surgeon say to the patient when he woke up?
"Oops, I didn't know you were still alive."

There's less to go until 250!

151. What does a dead lawyer do?
Prepare your defense in hell.

152. What did the coffin say to the tombstone?
"Thanks for having my back."

153. My boss said I could "die on the job."
I think I'll take your offer literally.

154. What's worse than forgetting someone?
Remember it just when it's too late.

155. Why does karma never rest?
Because he always has work to do with us.

156. What is a zombie doing in a bakery?
Ask if cakes have brains.

157. What did the sky say to the storm?
"Let me shine, you already have enough tears."

158. What is sadder than a goodbye?
A goodbye with no return.

159. What does an executioner do at Christmas?
Enjoy your gift list... and your convicts.

160. Why don't ballot boxes have wheels?

Because nobody wants the dead to continue traveling.

161. What is a corpse doing at a demonstration?
Giving body to the movement.

162. Why do arsonists never have a home?
Because they can't help but burn it.

163. My friend said he wanted to "sleep forever."
I got him a comfortable coffin.

164. What did the axe say to the executioner?
"Today we are going to break up with someone."

165. Why don't psychologists work in cemeteries?
Because there everyone has already solved their problems.

166. My grandmother always said: "Don't go near the fire."
Now I understand why when I see his urn.

167. What does a clown do at a funeral?
Making sure no one takes life too seriously.

168. Why don't the dead pay taxes?
Because they have already given their full share.

169. What did the ghost say to the mirror?
"Today you look emptier than I do."

170. My cousin became a suicide pilot.
I told him that at least he has a flight plan now.

171. What does an executioner do when he retires?
Practice clipping coupons.

172. What's worse than a bad day?
A bad day that ends forever.

173. What is a corpse doing in a laboratory?
Waiting for your turn to be useful one last time.

174. What did the skeleton say to the surgeon?
"Thanks for not leaving me hanging."

175.Why do zombies hate exams?
Because they always get zero in brain.

176.What's scarier than a funeral?
One you wake up in.

177.What do orphans do at Christmas?
Hope that Santa Claus doesn't forget them too.

178.Why are coffins so comfortable?
Because there are never any complaints from users.

179.What did the tombstone say to the corpse?
"I hope you like the shade."

180.What's worse than being fired?
Have your boss attend your funeral to make sure you don't come
back.

Coming to the end (181-250)

181.What is a ghost doing in a library?
Find stories that don't include it.

182.What did the executioner say to his date?
"I hope your head is on right side."

183.My neighbor always said:
"I'm going to shine someday." And boy did she when her house
burned down.

184.What is sadder than losing a friend?
Lose him twice if he comes back as a ghost.

185.Why are funerals so formal?
Because it's the last time anyone wears a suit.

186.What does a surgeon do in his spare time?
Practice on mannequins... and sometimes something else.

187.My friend wanted to donate his body to science.

Too bad science said, "No, thank you."

188. What do arsonists do at parties?
Light up the atmosphere, literally.

189. Why are coffins never on sale?
Because death is not negotiable.

190. My grandfather always said:
"You're leaving just as you came." That's why we buried him naked.

191. What did the devil say to the newcomer?
"Welcome home, friend."

192. What's scarier than a clown?
A dead clown who keeps smiling.

193. What did the doctor say to the terminally ill patient?
"Don't worry, there's no turning back."

194. My neighbor bought a climbing rope.
I guess he decided to use it differently.

195. What is a corpse doing at a wedding?
Celebrate that you don't have to go through that.

196. Why do orphans hate picture frames?
Because they never have family photos.

197. What does a firefighter do in hell?
He wonders where he left the hose.

198. Why are funerals so expensive?
Because it's the last luxury you'll ever have.

199. What does a suicidal person do with a bridge?
Measure the impact your decision will have.

200. What is crueler than an executioner?
One who takes his time.

Last 50 jokes to close

201.What's worse than losing hope?
   Losing your life while looking for it.

202.What did the corpse tell the coroner?
   "I hope you enjoy your work."

203.What is a ghost doing in a park?
   Take care of the banks... because he has nothing better to do.

204.What did karma say to the murderer?
   "We'll see you soon."

205.My friend decided to face the train.
   Guess who won.

206.Why don't psychologists commit suicide?
   Because they know there is always someone worse than them.

207.What is a dead person doing in a church?
   Waiting for a miracle that never comes.

208.What did the parachute say to the suicide bomber?
   "I didn't come here to save you."

209.What's worse than a bad day?
   A bad day that ends in the hospital.

210.What do orphans do when they grow up?
   Keep waiting for someone to choose them.

211.What is a lawyer doing in a cemetery?
   Taking care of your old customers.

212.What's worse than a ghost in the house?
   One who does not pay rent.

213.What did the empty tomb say to the new one?
   "There is always room for another."

214.Why are zombies bad at playing hide and seek?
   Because they always smell rotten.

215. My friend asked me to help him "get over a bridge."
Too bad he didn't specify how.

216. What did the skeleton say to the cemetery?
"I can finally rest in peace... or in pieces."

217. What's worse than losing a tooth?
Losing it while eating rocks to keep from crying.

218. My grandfather always said: "In life everything is temporary."
It's a pity he died in a bus accident.

219. What is an arsonist doing in a shelter?
Making sure everyone has a "warmth of home."

220. What did the surgeon tell the patient after the operation?
"I hope your insurance covers the mistakes."

221. What's scarier than a serial killer?
One that hasn't found you yet.

222. My neighbor said he was ready for the afterlife.
I replied: "Well, hurry up, you're taking up space here."

223. What is a child doing in a hospital without insurance?
Pray that the doctor doesn't mind.

224. What did the tombstone say to the corpse?
"I hope you'll be a good tenant."

225. What is a suicidal person doing in a rope store?
Buy the "deal of a lifetime".

226. What's worse than having no future?
Have it and it sucks.

227. What is a ghost doing with a chair?
Nothing, because he doesn't have a butt to sit on.

228. My friend said that life was a gift.
I said, "I hope they give you the return ticket."

229. What is a corpse doing in a morgue?

Practice for your big day.

230.What did the cemetery say to the hurricane?
"Leave me alone, I have enough mess here."

231.Why do orphans hate family soap operas?
Because they never understand the concept.

232.What does a suicidal pilot do on his last flight?
Make sure no one asks for applause when landing.

233.What did karma say to the liar?
"Don't worry, I have time for you."

234.My friend said he wanted to be an astronaut.
I replied: "Well, hurry up, you're already dead inside."

235.What does a retired executioner do?
Cutting down trees for Christmas.

236.What did the dead man say to the priest?
"Thanks for the words, but you arrived late."

237.What is a ghost doing at a wake?
Check who is really crying.

238.Why don't the dead complain about burials?
Because they have no options left.

239.My neighbor said he wanted to be unforgettable.
So I stole everything from him after his funeral.

240.What does a coffin on wheels do?
Waiting for a traveling corpse.

241.What did the skeleton say to the doctor?
"Be careful not to break anything, I'm barely whole!"

242.Why don't clowns go to hell?
Because the devil fears them.

243.What does a dead person do in a traffic accident?
Waiting for someone to call a tow truck... for him.

244. My friend wanted to save on the hospital.
So we buried him in the garden.

245. What is a ghost doing in an amusement park?
Scare those who are already scared.

246. Why don't psychologists work in funeral homes?
Because no one pays for therapy after they die.

247. My grandfather wanted to "fly away."
We misunderstood it and cremated it.

248. What did the coffin say to the corpse?
"Welcome to your new mobile home!"

249. What does a retired firefighter do?
Nothing, because it still burns inside.

250. My friend said his life was a tragedy.
I replied: "Relax, it can still be a comedy."

CLOWN DOWN

Very Cruel and Bizarre Jokes (1-250)

1-50

1. Why don't orphans wear watches?
   Because they don't have time to find a family.

2. My friend wanted to go to heaven…
   I told him, "First learn to detach yourself from the Earth."

3. What is a corpse doing in an amusement park?
   Try permanent free fall.

4. Why don't zombies eat at expensive restaurants?
   Because they prefer fast, cerebral food.

5. My cousin died searching for his purpose in life.
   At least he found the ground.

6. What did cancer tell its patient?
   "Relax, we're going to have a good time together."

7. My neighbor put a rope in his room.
   I guess he wanted to decorate… permanently.

8. What is an arsonist doing in a burn hospital?
   Take notes.

9. What's scarier than a surgeon with a bad pulse?
   One with good aim in the wrong place.

10. What did the coffin say to the dead man?
    "I'm going to squeeze you, but only because we're friends."

11. What does a clown do at a funeral?
    Steal the show…and the family memories.

12. My grandfather said he wanted to die in peace.
    That's why I stole his headphones before unplugging him.

13. Why don't orphans celebrate Christmas?
    Because Santa doesn't know where to leave them.

14. What does an amputee do with a glove?
    Use it as a hat.

15. What did the ghost say to the boy who couldn't sleep?
    "I can't either, welcome to my world!"

16. My neighbor told me: "I'm going to jump off the building."
    I replied: "Tell me when, so I can record it in slow motion."

17. What's worse than a slow death?
    A fast life that leads to nothing.

18. My friend wanted to donate his organs...
    But nobody wanted to accept them because of "misuse."

19. What is an arsonist doing in a nursing home?
    Prepare a "hot" party.

20. What's crueler than a black joke?
    A sharp knife in the wrong hands.

21. My ex said he would kill me.
    I replied: "Promise or threat?"

22. What is an orphan doing in a family contest?
    You are automatically disqualified.

23. My cousin got a tattoo saying "live every day as if it were your last."
    He died a week later.

24. What is a corpse doing at a wedding?
    Decorate the coldest corner of the room.

25. What did the guillotine say to the condemned man?
    "Don't worry, this will be quick."

26. What is an orphan doing in a hospital?
    Practicing how to not get chosen again.

27. My friend said he was not afraid of death.
    I said, "Go on, ask her to dance."

28. What did an evil clown say to a politician?
    "Teach me how to scare better."

29. My uncle wanted to be remembered forever.
    So we buried him in an unmarked grave.

30. What's worse than a fatal accident?
    Being the guilty survivor.

31. My friend got "indestructible" tattooed.
    He died after tripping on a sidewalk.

32. What is an arsonist doing in a forest?
    Organize an "unforgettable event".

33. What did the corpse tell the coroner?
    "I hope you are inspired today!"

34. What is a suicidal person doing on a bridge?
    Decorate the river with drama.

35. Why don't ghosts have children?
    Because there is no sperm in the afterlife.

36. What did the rope say to the suicide?
    "I got you, literally."

37. My friend asked me for some advice before taking the plunge.
    I told him: "Wear a helmet, the blow will be hard."

38. What does an amputee do with a watch?
    Use it as a mirror.

39. What did karma say to the murderer?
    "I'm coming for you, but I like to take my time!"

40. What is an orphan doing in a zoo?
    Adopt a monkey as a mother.

41. My neighbor said he wanted to "go far away."
    So I buried it in the backyard.

42. What did the knife say to the butcher?

"Thank you for making me famous."

43. What does an arsonist do at Christmas?
Give charcoal to everyone... handmade.

44. What is crueler than a happy executioner?
One who sings while working.

45. My grandfather wanted to be remembered as a hero.
That's why I pushed him in front of a moving bus.

46. What is a corpse doing in a freezer?
Waiting for his debut in the morgue.

47. What did the tombstone say to the dead man?
"I've got you covered, literally."

48. What does a brainless zombie do?
Looking for a job in human resources.

49. Why are clowns good killers?
Because they know how to hide bodies... and laughter.

50. My cousin always wanted to "burn his problems away."
Now his ashes are part of the wind.

Very Cruel and Bizarre Jokes (51-100)

51. My friend said he always felt empty.
So I helped him get into a coffin.

52. What does an orphan do on Family Day?
Asking to be adopted... again.

53. What did the water say to the suicide?
"Come, I'll be waiting for you with open arms."

54. My neighbor always said he wanted to fly.
I didn't know he meant that literally until I saw it on the pavement.

55. What did the knife say to the wrist of a suicide bomber?
"I hope you're ready for a definitive cut."

56. What does an arsonist do on New Year's?
    Create your own fireworks show.

57. What did the amputee say to the glove salesman?
    "I only need half, thanks."

58. My grandfather always wanted an epic funeral.
    So we hired a clown to dance on top of his coffin.

59. Why don't zombies visit the living?
    Because the living are always busy burying them.

60. What is a corpse doing in a freezer?
    Waiting to be the main course of an episode of CSI.

61. What did the butcher say to his apprentice?
    "I hope you have the stomach for this."

62. My cousin wanted to do something unforgettable.
    That's why they found it on the news.

63. What is a suicidal person doing on a cruise ship?
    Planning a plunge into the water... in style.

64. What's darker than black humor?
    My basement full of jokes that no one should tell.

65. My neighbor said he wanted to be unforgettable.
    Now his grave has more flowers than the park.

66. What does an amputee do with a long sleeve?
    Turns it into decoration.

67. What did the devil say to the sinner?
    "I hope you like the heat."

68. My friend said that life was a cruel joke.
    I replied, "Get ready for the punchline."

69. What is a ghost doing in a hospital?
    Find new friends to take to the other side.

70. Why do orphans hate family jokes?

Because they never understand the context.

71. What did the rope around the suicide's neck say?
    "Just relax, I'll do the rest."

72. My cousin always said he wanted to shine.
    He is now the main star of the local obituary.

73. What does a zombie do on a strict diet?
    Look for low-carb brains.

74. What did the coffin say to the corpse?
    "You look comfortable in there."

75. What does an executioner do on his day off?
    He sharpens his tools for fun.

76. My grandfather always said that heaven was his destiny.
    I didn't know you were referring to cremation.

77. What is an arsonist doing in a circus?
    Find the perfect excuse to set something on fire.

78. What's worse than losing a loved one?
    Finding it after having forgotten it.

79. What is a corpse doing on a beach?
    Practice eternal tanning.

80. My friend said he wanted to "leave his mark on the world."
    That's why he jumped from the highest building.

81. What does an amputee do in a race?
    Surprise everyone with your speed... on one wheel.

82. What did the knife say to the murderer?
    "Today we are going to make history."

83. My neighbor wanted to become famous.
    Now his photo is in the morgue as an example of what not to do.

84. What does a hungry zombie do?
    Decorate your plate with a fresh brain.

85. What did the wind say to the suicide?
    "Let me take care of the fall."

86. My grandfather wanted to "go big."
    So we hired fireworks for his cremation.

87. What is an arsonist doing in a nursing home?
    Make sure everyone has a "warm farewell."

88. Why are funerals so boring?
    Because the main guest never speaks.

89. What is a suicidal person doing in a tall building?
    Planning the most eye-catching landing of the year.

90. My friend said he wanted to rest in peace.
    That's why I buried him before he could change his mind.

91. What does an amputee do with an extra shoe?
    He uses it as a paperweight.

92. What did the coroner say to the corpse?
    "You are a fascinating puzzle."

93. What is a ghost doing in an airport?
    Find cheap flights to the underworld.

94. My neighbor always said it was indestructible.
    Until a flowerpot put it in its place.

95. What is an arsonist doing in a library?
    Decorate it with flames.

96. What did karma say to the sinner?
    "Don't worry, I'm already on my way."

97. What is a corpse doing in a park?
    Scare the fun-seekers.

98. My cousin wanted to "leave his mark on the world."
    There is now a memorial where it landed.

99. What does a zombie with a bad taste do?

Find a chef who will improve your diet.

100. What did the coffin say to the earth?
"Get ready for the deadlift."

Very Cruel and Bizarre Jokes (101-150)

101. What does an amputee do with an umbrella?
Use it as a walking stick when it's not raining.

102. My friend wanted "a new beginning."
Now her photo is in the obituary as a debutante.

103. What did the ground say to the suicide?
"Relax, I'll receive you."

104. What is an arsonist doing in a church?
Create a "burning miracle."

105. My grandfather always said: "Death doesn't hurt."
Now I understand why he never complained after he left.

106. What did the knife say to the butcher?
"Thank you for giving me purpose."

107. What is a corpse doing in a costume shop?
Find a suit that fits better.

108. Why don't zombies go to the gym?
Because they are always at their ideal weight: dead.

109. What did the tombstone say to the cemetery?
"Another satisfied customer!"

110. My neighbor always said: "I'm going to be unforgettable."
Now his photo is on every corner with a "wanted" tag.

111. What does a suicidal person do with an open window?
Let the breeze in... and out with it.

112. My friend said he would "never look down."
That's why he never saw the ground coming.

113.What did the water say to the floating corpse?
"Always adrift!"

114.What is an arsonist doing in a museum?
Create an ephemeral work of art.

115.Why do orphans hate musical chairs?
Because they always lose in the end.

116.My grandfather used to say that "everything returns to dust."
That's why we cremated him.

117.What did karma say to the liar?
"I hope you like the taste of your words."

118.What is a corpse doing in a hotel?
Rest forever in your last suite.

119.My friend said it was "unattainable."
That's why he jumped out of a plane without a parachute.

120.What does an amputee do with an old shoe?
He sells it to someone with both feet.

121.What did the coffin say to the cemetery?
"Fill out the guest list!"

122.Why don't zombies use condiments?
Because they prefer the natural taste of the brain.

123.My cousin always wanted to "travel light."
That's why his ashes are in a small box.

124.What is a corpse doing at a party?
Be the dead soul of the celebration.

125.What did the knife say to the suicide?
"Don't worry, this will only hurt once."

126.My grandfather always said that "life was short."
Too bad he took it too seriously.

127.What is an arsonist doing in an animal shelter?

Make sure everyone finds warmth quickly.

128.What did the ground say to the skydiver who forgot his equipment?
"I was waiting for you."

129.My neighbor always said he wanted to "go out with a bang."
Now his name is on a tombstone on a hilltop.

130.What is a zombie doing in a bakery?
Look for brain pies.

131.Why do ghosts never get lost?
Because they always find their way back to the cemetery.

132.What did the rope say to the suicide?
"This will be your last knot."

133.My friend wanted to become a star.
So they launched it into space... as a media disaster.

134.What is a corpse doing in a river?
Practice aquatic meditation.

135.What did the knife say to the butcher?
"Thank you for giving me a sharp purpose."

136.My grandfather wanted a memorable funeral.
So we threw it into the nearest volcano.

137.What is an arsonist doing in a national park?
Adding warmth to nature.

138.What did karma say to the murderer?
"We'll see each other very soon."

139.My friend said that life was a game.
I guess he lost the final game.

140.What is a zombie doing at a wake?
Recruit new friends.

141.What did the coffin say to the tombstone?

"We work as a team."

142. My neighbor always wanted to "live fast and die young."
The tree he crashed into also had similar plans.

143. What is a suicidal person doing on a roller coaster?
Change plans after the first turn.

144. My grandfather always said that words kill.
It's a shame he never went to the doctor because of the gunshot wounds he received.

145. What is a corpse doing in a nightclub?
Tearing up the track... literally.

146. What did the wind say to the suicide on the bridge?
"Come on, I'll give you a push!"

147. My cousin wanted a radical change in his life.
It is now part of the pavement.

148. What does an amputee do with extra socks?
It turns them into puppets.

149. What did karma say to the thief?
"I hope you enjoy your prize... for a little while."

150. My neighbor always said that airplanes were safe.
I guess he forgot his seatbelt when he got thrown out of one.

Very Cruel and Bizarre Jokes (151-200)

151. What is a corpse doing in a gym?
Lift weights... for the last time.

152. My friend always said he hated heights.
Now he rests in peace, six meters underground.

153. What did the knife say to the murderer?
"Today we will make art."

154. Why don't ghosts play hide and seek?
Because they are always transparent.

155. My cousin wanted "one last big jump."
It's a shame there was no net below.

156. What is a zombie doing in a hair salon?
Ask for a brain cut.

157. What did the tombstone say to the new tenant?
"I hope you are quiet."

158. My grandfather always said he wanted to be remembered.
Now he has his face on the cigarette pack that killed so many people.

159. What is an arsonist doing at a wedding?
Making sure everyone sees flames in love.

160. Why do orphans hate Disney movies?
Because they don't have a happy ending.

161. My neighbor always said he wanted to go to space.
Now his ashes are in orbit.

162. What does a suicidal person do with a tightrope?
He rehearses his final work.

163. What did the water say to the floating corpse?
"Finally someone who doesn't complain about my temperature."

164. My friend wanted to "go to the other side."
The bridge welcomed him with open arms.

165. What is a corpse doing in a library?
Stay in the same book forever.

166. What did karma say to the drunk driver?
"See you at the next post."

167. Why don't zombies diet?
Because they don't need to be alive to eat.

168. My grandfather always said he wanted to be free.
Now it is... in the form of scattered ashes.

169. What does a clown do at a wake?
Practice making someone cry for real.

170. What did the rope say to the suicide?
"Relax, I won't let you fall."

171. My friend always said he wanted to make history.
It is now the main topic in the crime newspaper.

172. What is a corpse doing in a freezer?
He makes sure not to melt down over problems.

173. What did the knife say to the butcher?
"Today we cut off dreams."

174. My neighbor always wanted to be a pilot.
Now his epitaph reads: "He flew high, but landed badly."

175. What is a zombie doing in a hospital?
Demand fresh brains from the operating rooms.

176. Why don't orphans look at family photos?
Because they are always empty albums.

177. What did the coffin say to the dead man?
"I got you, but don't expect much space."

178. My grandfather always said that fire was his friend.
That's why we cremated him with a smile.

179. What is a suicide doing in a skyscraper?
Plan your non-stop flight.

180. What did the tombstone say to the corpse?
"Welcome to the silent club."

181. What is an arsonist doing in an animal shelter?
Make sure everyone is "warm."

182. My friend said life was too short.
I replied, "That explains why you are in a hurry to finish it."

183. What is a corpse doing in a parade?

Decorate the float of the afterlife.

184.What did the wind say to the suicide on the bridge?
"Let me take you away."

185.My cousin always wanted to be part of something big.
Now it is... of the pavement.

186.What does an amputee do with extra gloves?
He gives halves to his friends.

187.What did karma say to the thief?
"Don't worry, I'm preparing something for you."

188.My neighbor always said that trees were strong.
Until one fell on him.

189.What is a zombie doing in a park?
Find distracted brains for lunch.

190.What did the knife say to the suicide?
"This will be quick... or not."

191.My grandfather always said he wanted to be ashes in the wind.
That's why we launched it with a fan on.

192.What is a corpse doing in a laboratory?
Participate in experiments without protest.

193.What did the water say to the corpse?
"Now we are friends forever."

194.My friend wanted to experience free fall.
Too bad he forgot his parachute.

195.What does an amputee do with a leftover shoe?
He turns it into a flower pot.

196.What did the coffin say to the cemetery?
"I bring you a new gift."

197.Why don't zombies wear glasses?
Because they no longer have eyes to focus.

198. My neighbor always wanted to work in construction.
Now it is part of the concrete.

199. What does a suicidal person do with an empty bridge?
Take a step into the abyss.

200. What did the tombstone say to the corpse?
"I'll take care of you, as long as you don't get up."

Very Cruel and Bizarre Jokes (201-250)

201. What is a corpse doing in a play?
Stealing the final act.

202. My grandfather always said that he wanted to "be one with nature."
That's why we buried him without a coffin.

203. What did the wind say to the suicide?
"Don't worry, I'll give you the final push."

204. My neighbor always said that boats were safe.
Until they found him floating next to one.

205. What is a zombie doing on a farm?
Search for organic brains.

206. Why do orphans hate group photos?
Because they never know where to stand.

207. What did the coffin say to the dead man?
"Don't move, the worst is over."

208. My cousin always wanted to learn to fly.
Too bad he forgot the landing part.

209. What is an arsonist doing in a fire station?
Looking for inspiration for your next fire.

210. What did the knife say to the butcher?
"I hope you enjoy what we are creating."

211. My friend always said he wanted to leave his mark on the world.

Now there is a stain on the pavement with his name.

212.What is a corpse doing in a swimming pool?
Enjoy your eternal bath.

213.Why don't zombies wear belts?
Because they always lose control of their pants... and limbs.

214.My grandfather wanted an epic ending.
So we cremated him during a fireworks show.

215.What is a suicidal person doing in a rope factory?
Compare options for your grand finale.

216.What did karma say to the liar?
"Don't worry, I'm already writing down your pending tasks."

217.My neighbor always said he was immortal.
I guess the lightning thought otherwise.

218.What is a zombie doing in a hospital?
Steals fresh brains silently.

219.Why don't orphans celebrate Mother's Day?
Because nobody sends them invitations.

220.What did the coffin say to the cemetery?
"I bring another satisfied customer."

221.My cousin always wanted to have a luxurious grave.
Now he has a golden cross that shines brighter than his life.

222.What is a corpse doing in a river?
Practice meditation... for life.

223.What did the knife say to the murderer?
"Today we will do something unforgettable."

224.My grandfather always said he wanted to "leave in style."
So we pushed him in his wheelchair down a hill.

225.What is a zombie doing in a library?
Look for books on cerebral gastronomy.

226. Why do orphans hate birthday parties?
Because they never know who to thank.

227. What did the tombstone say to the corpse?
"Don't worry, I'll cover you."

228. My neighbor wanted to be a movie star.
Now he is the protagonist of all the cemetery stories.

229. What is a suicide doing with a famous bridge?
He makes sure that his last act is unforgettable.

230. What did karma say to the irresponsible driver?
"I'm waiting for you around the next bend."

231. My friend always said he wanted to live fast.
Now his epitaph is the only one in bold.

232. What is a corpse doing in a freezer?
Practices for her CSI debut.

233. Why don't zombies use technology?
Because they prefer simple things... like brains.

234. My grandfather wanted to be unforgettable.
Now his urn is the centerpiece of the living room.

235. What is an arsonist doing in a paper mill?
Find the perfect fuel for your next job.

236. What did the knife say to the suicide?
"I hope you're ready to cut it all off."

237. My cousin always wanted to shine.
Now he does it every time someone cleans his tombstone.

238. What is a zombie doing in a supermarket?
Look for canned brains.

239. Why don't orphans watch superhero movies?
Because they never understand the concept of "family origin".

240. What did the coffin say to the cemetery?

"This will be my last delivery."

241.My grandfather always said that life was a roller coaster.
I guess he eventually got tired of the ups and downs.

242.What is a corpse doing in a morgue?
He waits patiently for his debut at the autopsy.

243.What did karma say to the corrupt politician?
"Prepare for an eternal mandate... in hell."

244.My neighbor always wanted to be remembered.
That's why we buried him with a statue that no one can ignore.

245.What is a zombie doing in a bakery?
Decorate a cake with marzipan brains.

246.What did the tombstone say to the dead man?
"I will keep your secrets... forever."

247.My cousin always wanted to go to the top of the world.
That's why we buried him on the highest mountain.

248.What is a corpse doing on a beach?
Enjoy a permanent tan.

249.What did the knife say to the butcher?
"Let's break the monotony, let's do something creative."

250.My grandfather always said: "Silence is golden."
I guess the cemetery is a mine of riches.

250 Jokes with Very Dark and Absurd Humor (1-250)

1-50

1. What is a corpse doing in the gym?
   Nothing, but he still lifts more than me.

2. My friend tried to commit suicide with a plastic knife.
   Now he has an appointment with the psychologist... and with the plastic surgeon.

3. What does a vegan zombie do?
   He chews grass while crying over his diet.

4. What did the blind man say when he was given a book in Braille?
   "Gross! Who left crumbs on the cover?"

5. Why don't orphans use GPS?
   Because they never find a place to call home.

6. My neighbor wanted to fly with an umbrella like Mary Poppins.
   Now they know it as "The Corner Disaster."

7. What is an arsonist doing in a nursing home?
   Blow out birthday candles... with a flamethrower.

8. My grandfather asked that we bury him with his dog.
   Too bad the dog was still alive.

9. What is a corpse doing in a mannequin factory?
   It confuses all the employees.

10. What did the fish say to the suicide on the bridge?
    "Watch out for crash landings, buddy!"

11. What is a sad clown doing at a wake?
    He tells bad jokes to cheer up the dead.

12. Why don't ghosts cross the street?
    Because they always get run over... again.

13. My cousin wanted to be part of something big.
    It is now buried in a crater.

14. What did the coffin say to the dead man?
    "Relax, this is just the beginning."

15. What is an arsonist doing in a plastic forest?
    An ecological disaster... and a logical one.

16. Why do orphans hate surprise parties?
    Because there is never anyone to surprise them.

17. What is a zombie doing in a yoga center?
    Practice the art of not moving.

18. My grandfather always said that coffee gave him life.
    Too bad the last one was with arsenic.

19. What does a suicide bomber do with a bungee cord?
    It becomes the spectacle of the park.

20. Why don't zombies have pets?
    Because they always eat them by mistake.

21. What did the tombstone say to the new corpse?
    "I hope you have good taste, because you'll be here a long time."

22. My neighbor wanted to build a homemade airplane.
    It is now buried alongside the remains of the fuselage.

23. What is a clown doing in a cemetery?
    Give out balloons to those who no longer need them.

24. Why don't dead people wear designer clothes?
    Because no one sees them on the other side.

25. My cousin wanted to be unforgettable.
    Now his photo is on every lamppost in the neighborhood.

26. What is an arsonist doing at a foam party?
    Turn it into a smoke party.

27. What did the ghost say to the exorcist?
    "Do you come with a guarantee?"

28. Why don't orphans have family albums?

Because they don't have any photos to fill them.

29. My friend wanted to be creative at his funeral.
    So we ordered fireworks for his cremation.

30. What is a zombie doing in a bakery?
    Look for marzipan brains.

31. What did the knife say to the butcher?
    "I hope you have the stomach for this."

32. Why ghosts don't need therapy?
    Because they have already left their problems behind... and their
    bodies.

33. My grandfather wanted to "go big."
    So we launched it with a cannon.

34. What is a suicide doing on a tightrope?
    Check if he/she has life insurance.

35. What is an arsonist doing in a candle shop?
    He buys all the merchandise and lights it at the entrance.

36. My neighbor wanted to be a superhero.
    Now they know him as "The Useless Man."

37. What did the coffin say to the cemetery?
    "This is my new tenant, take good care of him."

38. Why don't zombies go to concerts?
    Because they always end up chasing the drummer.

39. My cousin always said he wanted to shine.
    Now his tombstone has LED lights.

40. What is a corpse doing on an ice rink?
    Confuse the skaters.

41. What did the suicide tell the psychologist?
    "Relax, I just came to say goodbye."

42. Why do ghosts hate motion detectors?

Because they always give them away.

43. My grandfather wanted to "be useful after death."
So now it's fertilizer for the plants.

44. What is a zombie doing in a library?
Look for brain recipes.

45. What is an arsonist doing in a zoo?
Organize an "animal barbecue."

46. My neighbor wanted to enter heaven.
But he forgot to make an appointment.

47. What did the tombstone say to the coffin?
"Thank you for delivering this package to me."

48. Why don't orphans watch family movies?
Because they always remind them of what they don't have.

49. My cousin wanted to be remembered as someone unique.
Now his epitaph reads: "Here lies an unrepeatable disaster."

50. What is a suicidal person doing on an empty bridge?
Let the wind make the decision for him.

Very Dark and Absurd Humor Jokes (51-100)

51. What is a zombie doing at a birthday party?
He eats the clown because he thinks he's stuffed with candy.

52. My grandfather wanted to be cremated, but he left an ambiguous will.
Now his ashes are mixed with the family grill.

53. What did the rope say to the suicide?
"Don't worry, today we work as a team."

54. What is a corpse doing at a wedding?
Acts as a witness that "forever" is not always good.

55. Why do ghosts never have debts?
Because they always disappear before paying.

56. My cousin always said he wanted to fly.
    He is now the only frequent passenger on an air coffin.

57. What is a zombie doing in an amusement park?
    Try to bite the guy dressed as cotton candy.

58. What did the coffin say to the corpse?
    "I hope you like wood, because that's all you'll see."

59. My neighbor wanted to invent a time machine.
    He only managed to get ahead of his funeral.

60. Why do orphans hate treasure hunts?
    Because they never find what they are looking for.

61. What is an arsonist doing in a fire extinguisher factory?
    It tests your patience... and that of your employees.

62. My grandfather said he always wanted to be surrounded by nature.
    Now it is visited more by insects than people.

63. What is a corpse doing in a yoga class?
    Practice the "eternal rest" position.

64. Why don't zombies have houses?
    Because they prefer to live outdoors... literally.

65. My friend wanted to break a world record.
    He is now the person who fell off a building the fastest.

66. What is a ghost doing at a football game?
    He plays forward, but always fails because the ball goes through.

67. What did the knife say to the suicide?
    "Come on, cut your troubles."

68. My cousin always said he wanted to be immortal.
    Now his photo is on a tombstone that no one visits.

69. What is an arsonist doing in a bookstore?
    Looking for literary fuel.

70.Why don't ghosts exercise?
   Because they don't have muscles to tone.

71.My grandfather asked that we bury him with his car.
   Now the cemetery looks like a used car dealership.

72.What is a zombie doing in a supermarket?
   Look for brains in the frozen food section.

73.What did the tombstone say to the corpse?
   "Don't worry, I'll keep your secret."

74.My neighbor wanted to "go big."
   So his funeral included a cannon... literally.

75.What is a corpse doing in a costume shop?
   Confuse all buyers.

76.Why don't orphans celebrate Father's Day?
   Because they always end up looking for one.

77.What did the coffin say to the cemetery?
   "Another satisfied customer."

78.My friend always said he wanted to leave his mark on the world.
   His body is now buried in a public garden.

79.What is a zombie doing in a butcher shop?
   He eats the butcher and says it is "self-service".

80.What did the knife say to the butcher?
   "Today we are going to make an epic cut."

81.My grandfather said he wanted to be useful after death.
   It is now part of a lamp made from bones.

82.What does a suicidal person do with a jump rope?
   Practice for your final performance.

83.Why don't ghosts wear hats?
   Because they always fall.

84.My neighbor wanted to fly on his motorcycle.

Now the bike is better than him.

85. What is a corpse doing in a morgue?
Look forward to his debut in the next episode of CSI.

86. What did the tombstone say to the cemetery?
"Thank you for inviting me to the party."

87. My cousin always said he hated airplanes.
Now rest in peace... after one.

88. What is a zombie doing in a restaurant?
He bites the chef and calls it "the dish of the day."

89. What did the coffin say to the dead man?
"I promise there will be no more ups and downs."

90. My grandfather wanted to be a hero.
Now his story is the one most told at funerals.

91. What is an arsonist doing in a fireworks store?
Fulfill all your dreams in one go.

92. Why do zombies never take baths?
Because they love the "vintage" smell.

93. My friend always said he hated boring funerals.
That's why we hired a DJ for yours.

94. What is a corpse doing in an art class?
Pose for the most disturbing sculpture.

95. What did the knife say to the murderer?
"You are an artist, and I am your paintbrush."

96. My grandfather wanted an unforgettable funeral.
So we held an auction for his coffin.

97. What is a zombie doing in a gym?
Look for brains in the snack machine.

98. What did the tombstone say to the corpse?
"I hope you don't snore."

99. My cousin wanted to write a book about near-death experiences.
He finished it just in time to live the last one.

100. What is a suicidal person doing in a circus?
Audition for the final act.

Very Dark and Absurd Humor Jokes (101-150)

101. What is a zombie doing in a Starbucks?
Order a coffee with brains, but no sugar.

102. My grandfather always said he wanted a discreet tombstone.
So we buried him with a "Do Not Disturb" sign.

103. What is a corpse doing in a library?
It becomes the dead literature section.

104. Why do ghosts hate modern houses?
Because the glass walls don't let them scare anyone.

105. My neighbor wanted to build a homemade rocket.
It is now buried alongside the wreckage of the failed launch.

106. What is an arsonist doing in a mattress store?
Test which ones burn best.

107. What did the rope say to the suicide?
"This will be an eternal bond."

108. My cousin always said he wanted to "live on the edge."
Now its limit is marked with flowers on a dangerous curve.

109. What is a zombie doing in a hair salon?
Look for brain extensions.

110. Why don't orphans watch Christmas movies?
Because there is never a happy ending for them.

111. What did the coffin say to the dead man?
"I will give you the rest you deserve... or the one you don't."

112. My friend wanted to jump off a building and survive.
Now they know it as "The Miracle of the Pavement."

113. What is a corpse doing in a zoo?
It becomes the new habitat of insects.

114. What did the knife say to the butcher?
"Today we will cut out even the excuses."

115. My grandfather always said that he wanted to be useful after death.
So we turn it into fertilizer for the plants.

116. What is a zombie doing in a gym?
Look for fresh brains among those who do not wear helmets.

117. Why don't ghosts drive cars?
Because they always go through the seat.

118. My neighbor wanted to be immortal.
Now his photo is all over the news... like an unsolved case.

119. What is an arsonist doing at a carnival?
Set fire to the most dangerous ride to up the excitement.

120. What did the tombstone say to the cemetery?
"Thank you for making me feel at home."

121. My cousin wanted to swim in a dangerous river.
Now the river bears his name.

122. What is a corpse doing in a play?
He steals the show by being the most convincing "extra."

123. What did the water say to the suicide?
"I promise it won't hurt... for long."

124. My friend wanted to be creative in his death.
Now his epitaph reads: "Here lies one who tried."too much".

125. What is a zombie doing in a hospital?
Steals brains straight from the operating room.

126. Why do ghosts hate vacuum cleaners?
Because they always feel trapped by them.

127. My grandfather asked that we cremate him with his favorite cigars.
Now your urn smells like your living room.

128. What is a corpse doing in a museum?
It becomes the exhibition of "past life".

129. What did the knife say to the suicide?
"I hope you're ready for this final cut."

130. My neighbor wanted to make history.
Now his house is a tourist site of tragedies.

131. What is a zombie doing in a cereal store?
Look for something that says "with real brains."

132. What did the coffin say to the dead man?
"This will be the most comfortable you'll ever be... forever."

133. My friend wanted to leave one last impression.
There is now a crater in the sidewalk named after him.

134. What is an arsonist doing in a supermarket?
Test how flammable each hallway is.

135. Why don't orphans have pets?
Because they always end up alone, just like them.

136. What did the tombstone say to the corpse?
"I hope you like the view."

137. My grandfather always said that life was like a flame.
Now he rests as ashes in an urn.

138. What is a zombie doing in a funeral home?
It confuses customers.

139. What did the knife say to the butcher?
"Let's cut it all off... no regrets."

140. My cousin wanted to jump out of a plane without a parachute.
Now it's in the record books... and on the ground.

141. What is a corpse doing at a concert?
    He is the only person who does not applaud at the end.

142. What did the coffin say to the cemetery?
    "This place is always packed, I like it."

143. My neighbor wanted to try urban skydiving.
    There is now a memorial in his name... next to the building.

144. What is a zombie doing at a party?
    Search for brains while everyone else eats snacks.

145. Why do ghosts hate mirrors?
    Because they never look good in them.

146. My grandfather asked for a low-key funeral.
    That's why we buried him in the backyard.

147. What is a corpse doing in a mannequin store?
    Fit perfectly.

148. What did the knife say to the suicide?
    "This will be easier than you think."

149. My cousin wanted to learn to swim in the deepest river.
    Now your body is part of the ecosystem.

150. What is a zombie doing in a cooking class?
    Ask for recipes for grilled brains.

Very Dark and Absurd Humor Jokes (151-200)

151. What is a zombie doing in a movie theater?
    He eats the person who speaks during the movie.

152. My grandfather always said: "Life is like a train, always onmotion".
    He didn't know that his end would be on the tracks.

153. What did the rope say to the suicide?
    "I am the knot that will never let you go."

154. Why don't orphans use maps?

Because they never find their way home.

155. My cousin wanted to be a firefighter, but he hated the water.
So he set his own truck on fire.

156. What is a corpse doing in an amusement park?
It's the only attraction that never screams.

157. What did the coffin say to the dead man?
"Welcome to your new apartment... without windows."

158. My friend wanted to make a documentary about death.
Now he is the protagonist.

159. What is a zombie doing in a flower shop?
Look for brains with a natural aroma.

160. Why do ghosts hate elevators?
Because they always get trapped between floors.

161. My grandfather wanted to "go with style."
So we launched it on a catapult into the ocean.

162. What is an arsonist doing in a fireworks factory?
Explodes with emotion... literally.

163. What did the knife say to the butcher?
"Today we will cut more than meat."

164. My neighbor always said he hated airplanes.
Now he's buried after trying one... for the last time.

165. What is a corpse doing in a hospital?
Inspire doctors to do better.

166. What did the tombstone say to the cemetery?
"Always full, never empty."

167. My cousin wanted to learn to fly.
Now his name is engraved in the ground.

168. What is a zombie doing in an art class?
It becomes the most realistic model.

169. Why don't ghosts eat fast food?
Because it passes through their bodies.

170. My grandfather asked to be buried with his guitar.
Now the roots of the tree touch better than he does.

171. What is a corpse doing in a gym?
He makes sure that no one loses the rhythm... of their heartbeats.

172. What did the coffin say to the dead man?
"At least you don't have to pay rent."

173. My friend wanted to jump off a famous bridge.
Now it has a commemorative plaque... and its name on the river.

174. What is a zombie doing in a bookstore?
Look for recipe books from gourmet brains.

175. Why don't ghosts have watches?
Because time no longer means anything to them.

176. My neighbor always said that life was an experiment.
It turns out that his was a failure.

177. What is a corpse doing on an athletics track?
He is the only one who never loses his position.

178. What did the knife say to the suicide?
"Today we cut off more than just problems."

179. My cousin wanted to be remembered forever.
Now his tombstone is a work of art... unintentional.

180. What is a zombie doing in a biology class?
Look for fresh brains under the microscope.

181. Why do orphans hate superhero movies?
Because they never have a familiar ending.

182. My grandfather wanted an epic funeral.
So we threw it into the nearest volcano.

183. What is a corpse doing in a yoga class?

Practice the "eternal rest" pose.

184. What did the tombstone say to the new corpse?
"I hope you'll be a quiet neighbor."

185. My friend wanted to experience an extreme jump.
Now the ground is the only thing that remembers it.

186. What is a zombie doing in a sushi restaurant?
Order brain sashimi.

187. Why don't ghosts wear shoes?
Because they always lose the sole.

188. My grandfather wanted to be cremated.
It is now in an urn that we use as decoration.

189. What is a corpse doing in an antique shop?
It blends perfectly with the relics.

190. What did the knife say to the butcher?
"Today we will make legendary cuts."

191. My cousin wanted to dive without equipment.
It is now part of the reef.

192. What is a zombie doing in a shelter?
Find free brains.

193. Why do ghosts hate LED lights?
Because they are too bright for his gloomy tastes.

194. My neighbor wanted to try skydiving with an umbrella.
Now the umbrella is in better shape than he is.

195. What is a corpse doing in a morgue?
He is patiently awaiting his next autopsy.

196. What did the coffin say to the cemetery?
"This customer won't complain about anything."

197. My friend wanted to innovate with his death.
Now his tombstone has a QR code.

198. What is a zombie doing in a technology store?
Look for USB brains.

199. Why do orphans hate family games?
Because they never have anyone to play them with.

200. What did the tombstone say to the dead man?
"I will take care of you better than life ever did."

Very Dark and Absurd Humor Jokes (201-250)

201. What is a zombie doing in a health food store?
Look for "organic" brains.

202. My grandfather always said that he wanted a quiet life.
Now it's quieter than ever, underground.

203. What did the knife say to the butcher?
"Today we will become a masterpiece of dismemberment."

204. What is a corpse doing in a spa?
Enjoy an advanced conservation treatment.

205. Why don't ghosts use umbrellas?
Because the rain never touches them.

206. My neighbor wanted to be an astronaut.
Now his ashes are scattered through space... thanks to the wind.

207. What is a zombie doing at a music festival?
Look for brains among those who dance the worst.

208. What did the coffin say to the dead man?
"I've got you covered forever."

209. My cousin always said that he hated routine.
That's why his tombstone is decorated in a unique way: with emojis.

210. What is a dead body doing in a water park?
It scares swimmers when it floats.

211. What did the tombstone say to the cemetery?

"Thanks for this new roommate."

212.My friend wanted to BASE jump from a skyscraper.
He forgot his parachute, but not his positive attitude.

213.What is a zombie doing in a coffee shop?
Order a coffee with extra brains.

214.Why do ghosts hate fans?
Because they always keep them away from their rooms.

215.My grandfather wanted us to always remember him.
That's why his tombstone plays audio every time you visit it.

216.What is a corpse doing in a biology class?
It is the most requested model.

217.What did the knife say to the suicide?
"Come on, let's make this moment unforgettable."

218.My neighbor wanted to become an urban hero.
Now his name decorates a plaque on the ground.

219.What is a zombie doing at a rock concert?
Look for brains among those who shake their heads too hard.

220.Why don't orphans watch romantic comedies?
Because they always end up crying for happy families.

221.My cousin always said he wanted to fly high.
Too bad all he got was a direct flight to the ground.

222.What is a corpse doing in a cooking class?
It becomes the "secret" ingredient.

223.What did the coffin say to the cemetery?
"Another satisfied customer for your collection."

224.My friend wanted to try free falling from an airplane.
His epitaph reads: "At least I tried."

225.What is a zombie doing in a perfume store?
Look for fresh brain fragrances.

226.Why don't ghosts wear watches?
Because they live in a timeless eternity.

227.My grandfather asked for his urn to have wheels.
Now we walk him like he's a pet.

228.What is a corpse doing in an art gallery?
It becomes the most realistic work.

229.What did the knife say to the butcher?
"Together, we can cut through any obstacle."

230.My neighbor wanted to innovate with his funeral.
Now there is a live stream from the cemetery.

231.What is a zombie doing in a toy store?
Find some plastic brains to practice with.

232.Why do ghosts hate LED bulbs?
Because they are too bright for his gloomy taste.

233.My cousin always said he loved the ocean.
Now his ashes are part of the waves.

234.What is a corpse doing at a fashion show?
It is the perfect model for the "post-mortem" collection.

235.What did the tombstone say to the dead man?
"Don't worry, everything is under control here."

236.My friend wanted to break an endurance record.
Now his name is engraved on a rock.

237.What is a zombie doing in a bread factory?
He's looking for brains to spread like butter.

238.Why do orphans hate Pixar movies?
Because they always have parents in the end.

239.My grandfather wanted to be remembered as a simple man.
That's why his tombstone has only a QR code that leads to his
story.

240. What is a corpse doing in a math class?
Solve the final equation of life.

241. What did the knife say to the suicide?
"Let's get this over with."

242. My neighbor always said he wanted to be a star.
Now his name is engraved on a monument in his memory.

243. What is a zombie doing in an appliance store?
Look for blenders for your brain smoothies.

244. Why don't ghosts need air conditioning?
Because they are always fresh.

245. My cousin wanted to innovate in extreme sports.
There is now a competition named in his honour.

246. What is a corpse doing in a clothing store?
Try the "dead elegant" outfits.

247. What did the coffin say to the cemetery?
"Always full, never boring!"

248. My friend wanted to turn his funeral into a spectacle.
Now he is the only one with a laser light show on his grave.

249. What is a zombie doing in a fancy restaurant?
Look for brains "al dente".

250. What did the tombstone say to the dead man?
"Relax, no one will ever bother you here."

250 Very Black and Cruel Political and Social Humor Jokes

1-50

1. What do politicians and zombies have in common?
   Both feed on brains... although politicians are always hungry.

2. My country is so screwed that if you find a bill on the street, it's probably fake... and from your own government.

3. Why don't congressmen have nightmares?
   Because their lives are already one.

4. Politicians always promise to lower taxes... and then they pull down your pants too.

5. What is a corrupt president doing in heaven?
   He makes sure that no one else comes in.

6. How do you know a politician is lying?
   Because his lips are moving.

7. In my country there are two types of politicians: those who steal... and those who have not yet learned how to do it.

8. What do banks and funeral homes have in common?
   They both thrive when you die.

9. My neighbor wanted to enter politics to do good.
   Now he's in prison for doing too well... for himself.

10. Why don't politicians need light in Congress?
    Because they are already working in the dark.

11. In my country, politicians have no ideology. They have bank accounts.

12. What did the voter say to the politician after the election?
    "Thank you for keeping your promises... of making my life impossible."

13. My country is so corrupt that even ghosts pay bribes to scare people.

14. What is the first thing a politician does when he comes to power?
Find where to put your mansion.

15. Banks don't go bankrupt. They only go bankrupt you.

16. Why are political speeches like soap operas?
Because they never make sense, but everyone still sees them.

17. How do you know your country is bankrupt?
When the central bank uses Monopoly to print money.

18. My president is so charismatic that even hell made him an offer to be an ambassador.

19. Why do politicians never go to the doctor?
Because their diagnoses always say "insensitive and heartless."

20. In my country, if you work hard, you can go far. Especially if you're running away from taxes.

21. What does a president do in a crisis?
Blame the previous president.

22. My country is so in debt that if I were to die, the world would still be charging interest.

23. What do a politician and a contortionist have in common?
They both know how to bend to fit into any situation.

24. Why shouldn't the poor vote?
Because they always choose someone who will make them poorer.

25. In my country, human rights are optional... but taxes are not.

26. My friend wanted to be a politician to change the world.
Now he lives in a mansion, and the world remains the same.

27. What does a politician do with honesty?
He buries her and collects taxes on the grave.

28. Why are laws like jokes?
Because they always benefit the one who tells them.

29. My country is so backward that we are still waiting for the democracy they bought to be returned to us.

30. What is worse than a dictator?
A dictator with Instagram.

31. Why are hospitals full during election times?
Because everyone gets sick of hearing so many promises.

32. My country has so much unemployment that even ghosts are lining up to haunt houses.

33. What do taxes and death have in common?
Both are inevitable, but taxes come first.

34. Why do politicians never learn from history?
Because they are too busy writing it in their favor.

35. My country is so corrupt that even dogs have offshore accounts.

36. Why do banks love economic crises?
Because they always get the best part.

37. My president promised to reduce poverty. And he kept his promise: now we are poor and unemployed.

38. What do a dictator and a comedian have in common?
Both make you laugh, but the dictator makes you laugh.

39. What did an honest politician say to a corrupt one?
"We don't exist, my friend!"

40. My country is so divided that the only unity is to steal together.

41. What does a politician do when he is caught stealing?
He is running for president.

42. In my country, judges do not dictate sentences, they dictate prices.

43. Why do the rich always win elections?
Because they buy the votes before you count them.

44. My neighbor ran for office.

I asked him if it was out of vocation or desperation. He said, "Because of the bank account."

45.What does a politician do with the poor?
He uses them as an excuse to get richer.

46.In my country, taxes are like vampires: they suck everything from you except your blood.

47.What do a bank and a casino have in common?
You lose in both, but the casino at least gives you drinks.

48.Why do dictators hate the ballot box?
Because they remind them that they are not immortal.

49.My president said he would take us into the future.
I didn't know that the future was full of debt.

50.What do a politician and a magician have in common?
They both distract you while taking everything you have.

Very Black and Cruel Political and Social Humor Jokes (51-100)

51.My country is so corrupt that when a politician is arrested, the judge gives him the option of "continuing where he left off or starting over."

52.Why are congressmen always safe in wars?
Because no one dares to fight for anything other than their money.

53.My president said he would end crime.
Now all the criminals are in his office.

54.What do dictators and unlicensed doctors have in common?
They both experiment regardless of the consequences.

55.My country is so poor that the only constant export is itscitizens.

56.Why are roads always under construction?
Because contracts are infinite, like corruption.

57.What does a politician do with a new hospital?

He turns it into a shopping mall, because health does not make money.

58. My neighbor wanted to be mayor to make things better.
He now lives in a gated community... with bodyguards.

59. What do banks and prisons have in common?
Both catch those who cannot pay.

60. My country has so many crises that children play at being economists to scare each other.

61. Why do the poor always lose elections?
Because their vote is cheap and easy to manipulate.

62. My president promised free education.
And he delivered: now we are all learning lessons from the crisis.

63. What does a politician do when he has no excuses?
Invent a new crisis to distract everyone.

64. In my country, corruption is like the air: it is everywhere, but no one can stop it.

65. What does a bank do when it can't collect payment from you?
It sells you to another bank so they can keep trying.

66. My neighbor wanted to be a union member to defend workers.
Now he defends his yacht bought with installments.

67. Why do politicians love long speeches?
Because the more they talk, the less they do.

68. My country is so in debt that even the rats took their things to emigrate.

69. What do dictators do when they die?
They become statues to continue oppressing from the grave.

70. My president promised to create jobs.
And he succeeded: now we all work in his family businesses.

71. What do politicians and religious pastors have in common?

Both promise a paradise that they never deliver.

72. In my country, elections are not democratic: they are popularity contests with bribes.

73. Why are judges always so calm?
Because they already collected before the trial.

74. My neighbor wanted to be a community leader.
He is now the leader of a pyramid scheme.

75. What does a bank do when you close your account?
He sends you a credit card to trick you into falling for it again.

76. In my country, the only time you see justice is when someone draws it in a cartoon.

77. What does one corrupt politician say to another?
"Share, my friend, there is something for everyone here."

78. My president promised to improve working conditions.
Now we all have three jobs to survive.

79. What do taxes and loans have in common?
They both haunt you to the grave.

80. In my country, if you report corruption, they make you part of it so you stay quiet.

81. What does an honest politician do?
Nothing, because it does not exist.

82. My neighbor ran for council saying he would make history.
And he succeeded: he is the first to be imprisoned before taking office.

83. Why do politicians never resign?
Because it is difficult to leave such a comfortable position.

84. In my country, inflation is so high that banknotes come with an expiration date.

85. What do dictators and arsonists have in common?

They both enjoy watching everything burn.

86. My president promised security.
    And he did: now the citizens are locked up while the thieves are free.

87. What does a bank do when it can't make any more money?
    Invent commissions for breathing.

88. In my country, if you work too much, you end up paying more taxes than the president.

89. What do unions do when there are labor problems?
    They negotiate so that the leaders get the best part.

90. My neighbor wanted to go on strike.
    Now he works double shifts to pay the fines.

91. Why do politicians love crises?
    Because they are the perfect excuse to steal more.

92. In my country, education is so bad that politicians seem intelligent.

93. What does a corrupt judge say to an accused politician?
    "Don't worry, this is just a formality."

94. My president said he would fight poverty.
    And he did: now everyone is equally poor.

95. What do the rich do in times of crisis?
    They change countries while others continue fighting.

96. In my country, banks are so kind that they offer you debts rather than advice.

97. What does a politician do when he loses support?
    Blame social media for telling the truth.

98. My neighbor wanted to protest against taxes.
    Now he has to pay even more for being "disobedient."

99. What do a dictator and a magician have in common?
    They both make things disappear, but the dictator never returns

them.

100. In my country, the only revolution that happens is when prices go up.

Very Black and Cruel Political and Social Humor Jokes (101-150)

101. What does a politician do when he receives criticism?
He opens a new offshore account to distract himself.

102. My president promised transparency.
Now we all see him steal in real time.

103. Why are election promises like diets?
Because everyone knows they won't come true.

104. In my country, if you study to be a politician, the degree includes an advanced course on tax evasion.

105. What does a bank do with your money?
It multiplies it... but for its managers.

106. My neighbor wanted to protest against corruption.
Now he is the only unemployed person in his neighborhood.

107. Why don't judges have mirrors at home?
Because they cannot look at each other after passing sentences they have bought.

108. My president promised to end hunger.
And he succeeded: now we are all too in debt to eat.

109. What do dictators and broken watches have in common?
They are both out of time, but still setting the pace.

110. In my country, the only place you find equality is in the graves.

111. What does a politician do when he gets bored in Congress?
Find new ways to make your life more expensive.

112. My neighbor ran for mayor saying he would fight corruption.
Now he has a mansion that proves otherwise.

113. Why do unions never lose?
Because they always negotiate for themselves, not for the workers.

114. In my country, the laws are so confusing that lawyers need lawyers to understand them.

115. What do banks do with small businesses?
They turn them into souvenirs, after seizing them.

116. My president said that the rich should pay more taxes.
That's why all the rich people live abroad now.

117. Why do politicians hate archives?
Because they always contain the evidence that sinks them.

118. In my country, elections are like lotteries: those who don't need the prize always win.

119. What does a corrupt judge do in his spare time?
He dispenses "justice" at private dinners with politicians.

120. My neighbor wanted to be a deputy to change things.
Now he changed his car, house and bank account.

121. Why do banks offer loans easily?
Because they know you can never give them back.

122. In my country, taxes are so high that happiness is also taxed.

123. What does a politician do when he can't make more money?
He is running for a higher position.

124. My president promised to create jobs.
Now we all work to survive, but not to live.

125. What do a dictator and a hacker have in common?
They both control everything from the dark.

126. In my country, inflation is so high that we use banknotes to wallpaper the walls.

127. What does an honest politician do?

It becomes a meme because no one takes it seriously.

128.My neighbor wanted to report electoral fraud.
Now his house is for sale because no one believed him.

129.Why do politicians love NGOs?
Because they are perfect for laundering money for a social cause.

130.In my country, political speeches are like reality shows: they make you laugh, cry and get angry... all at the same time.

131.What does a bank do when you win the lottery?
He calls you to offer you ways to lose it all.

132.My president said he would reduce poverty.
And he delivered: now we are all equally poor.

133.Why do judges never have money problems?
Because they always know how to negotiate sentences.

134.In my country, corruption is so common that it is already part of the national anthem.

135.What does a politician do in a crisis?
He turns it into an opportunity... to get richer.

136.My neighbor wanted to organize a peaceful protest.
He is now in prison for "public disorder."

137.Why are unions always on strike?
Because they need to justify their quotas.

138.In my country, the only way to get justice is to lose everything in the attempt.

139.What does a bank do when you go bankrupt?
He offers you another loan to sink you even further.

140.My president said he would invest in education.
Now we are all learning to live with less.

141.What do dictators and magicians have in common?
They both make everything go away, but it never comes back.

142. In my country, elections are like storms: they always end up leaving a disaster.

143. What does a politician do when he loses?
He becomes a news analyst to continue making a living from the system.

144. My neighbor wanted to be a senator to change the laws.
Now he has traded his cars for an armored one... just in case.

145. Why do banks never lose?
Because they always have more rules than you.

146. In my country, the only revolution that is moving forward is that of prices.

147. What does a corrupt judge do in a difficult case?
Find out who pays the most for their decision.

148. My president promised to improve public health.
Now we all exercise... to escape medical debt.

149. What do politicians and charlatans have in common?
They both offer you something they never deliver.

150. In my country, justice is blind... and deaf, and mute, and very expensive.

Very Black and Cruel Political and Social Humor Jokes (151-200)

151. What does a politician do when he receives a donation for works?public?
A swimming pool is built in his house.

152. My president said he would make education more accessible.
Now children learn about economics by selling gum on the streets.

153. Why banks don't need marketing?
Because they already have your money, whether you like it or not.

154. In my country, congressmen work so much... that even their excuses have overtime.

155.What does a politician do when he runs out of arguments?
He blames the opposition for inventing fake news.

156.My neighbor wanted to report corruption in his public company.
Now he is in the cleaning department.

157.Why do judges love high-profile cases?
Because they always gain more fame... and more money.

158.In my country, politicians are like meteorologists: they always promise change, but it never comes true.

159.What does a bank do when you can't pay?
They offer you a loan with higher interest to "help you out."

160.My president promised to reduce inequality.
And he succeeded: now we are all equally miserable.

161.What do politicians and stray bullets have in common?
Both always impact those who least deserve it.

162.In my country, the only transparency you see is that of your empty pockets.

163.What does a politician do when someone calls him a thief?
He replies: "That is defamation... and it is also true."

164.My neighbor wanted to be an activist to save the planet.
He now lives in an ecological cell.

165.Why do unions never achieve real improvements?
Because they always negotiate their profits first.

166.In my country, electoral promises are like rainbows: beautiful, but unattainable.

167.What does a corrupt judge do when he is investigated?
Ask for paid vacation.

168.My president promised a better future.
I didn't know he was referring to his family's future in another country.

169. What do banks and prisons have in common?
Both have bars... but the banks are more dangerous.

170. In my country, taxes are so high that even happiness is taxed.

171. What does a politician do when there are protests in the streets?
Increase your personal security... and your taxes.

172. My neighbor wanted to report a corrupt politician.
Now they call him "the missing one."

173. Why do dictators love history books?
Because they always rewrite them in their favor.

174. In my country, democracy is as real as a unicorn.

175. What does a bank do when you close your account?
He sends you a letter saying "we miss you" while you are being foreclosed on.

176. My president said he would protect workers.
I didn't know he was only talking about his own.

177. What do politicians and pirates have in common?
They both loot, but the pirates at least disguise themselves.

178. In my country, election campaigns are like weddings: expensive, exaggerated and full of lies.

179. What does a corrupt judge do with justice?
He sells it to the highest bidder.

180. My neighbor wanted to organize a workers' strike.
Now he's blacklisted... and unemployed.

181. Why do banks always offer new products?
Because they need more ways to make you poor.

182. In my country, inflation is so high that banknotes come with a survival manual.

183. What does an honest politician do?
Resign before they corrupt you.

184. My president promised equality for all.
And he delivered: now nobody has anything.

185. What do taxes and fines have in common?
They both exist only to make you suffer.

186. In my country, campaign promises are like fireworks: they shine for a moment and then disappear.

187. What does a corrupt judge do with a difficult case?
He files it away until he gets paid enough.

188. My neighbor wanted to create a movement against the banks.
Now we call him "the mortgaged one."

189. Why do politicians hate journalists?
Because they are the only ones who dare to tell the truth... sometimes.

190. In my country, human rights are like unicorns: everyone mentions them, but no one has seen them.

191. What does a politician do when he loses popularity?
Change your name and apply again.

192. My president said he would end poverty.
And it did: now poverty has finished us off.

193. What do banks and casinos have in common?
In both you lose, but at least the casino gives you a show.

194. In my country, the only wealth you see is that of politicians on their social media.

195. What does a corrupt judge do on his days off?
He invests in cases that he himself closed.

196. My neighbor wanted to run as an independent.
He is now affiliated with the party with the most money.

197. Why are politicians always smiling?
Because they know you never will.

198.In my country, education is so bad that memes teach more than teachers.

199.What does a bank do when you collect your salary?
They send you a message reminding you that you owe them.

200.My president promised to protect citizens.
And he did it: now we are protected at home because we cannot go out.

Very Black and Cruel Political and Social Humor Jokes (201-250)

201.What does a politician do when no one believes in his promises?
It promises more things, but with longer words.

202.My president promised to be the leader of change.
And he did: he moved his fortune to a tax haven.

203.Why are banks always building new buildings?
To save all the money that will never be returned to you.

204.In my country, social security is so secure... that it never reaches those who need it.

205.What does a politician do with emergency funds?
Makes sure your home is first in "emergency."

206.My neighbor wanted to start a charity.
He is so rich now that he should give himself away.

207.Why do corrupt judges not believe in justice?
Because they themselves destroy it.

208.In my country, political speeches are like blackouts: they come without warning and always leave you in the dark.

209.What does a bank do when you can't pay your mortgage?
He sends you a congratulatory card for your efforts before he evicts you.

210.My president promised to lower taxes.
And he did: he transferred them directly to our bank accounts.

211.What do dictators and social media have in common?
They both eliminate any voice they don't like.

212.In my country, democracy is like a lottery ticket: everyone buys it, but no one wins.

213.What does a politician do when he is caught stealing?
He holds a press conference to blame the opposing party.

214.My neighbor wanted to be an environmental activist.
Now they are looking for it because it disappeared faster than the Amazon.

215.Why are unions always in "negotiations"?
Because they need time to prepare their vacation.

216.In my country, laws change faster than the seasons.

217.What does a corrupt judge do when he receives a great offer?
He makes sure that the case closes with a flourish.

218.My president promised to improve infrastructure.
Now his house has an Olympic-sized swimming pool.

219.What do banks and sharks have in common?
They both smell blood from miles away.

220.In my country, politicians do not age: they simply changecharge to continue stealing.

221.What does a politician do when he loses an election?
Create a "citizen movement" to stay relevant.

222.My neighbor wanted to fight for equality.
Now we are all equally poor... except him.

223.Why dictators don't need friends?
Because they always have an army to back them up.

224.In my country, education is so poor that politicians seem intelligent.

225.What does a bank do with debts you can't pay?

He sells them to another bank to ensure that the harassment continues.

226. My president said he would work for the people.
I didn't know that "work" meant buying mansions in his name.

227. What do politicians and sundials have in common?
Both only work when everything is illuminated in their favor.

228. In my country, elections are like soap operas: full of drama, betrayal and disappointing endings.

229. What does a corrupt judge do when he wants to get promoted?
Makes sure to close cases... for the right price.

230. My neighbor wanted to organize a protest against inequality.
Now he is the only one in his neighborhood with a criminal record.

231. Why do banks never lose in crises?
Because they always make you foot the bill.

232. In my country, inflation is so high that banknotes come with a survival manual.

233. What does an honest politician do?
Quit before you get caught doing something good.

234. My president promised to end poverty.
And he succeeded: now we are all equally poor.

235. What do taxes and kidnappings have in common?
In both cases you pay, but you get nothing in return.

236. In my country, campaign promises are like unicorns: beautiful, but non-existent.

237. What does a corrupt judge do when he runs out of cases?
He creates new legal problems to keep himself busy.

238. My neighbor wanted to open an honest business.
Now he pays so much tax that his business no longer exists.

239. Why do politicians hate public debates?

Because they can't use their excuse book.

240. In my country, justice is like public Wi-Fi: slow, insecure and always failing.

241. What does a politician do when his country enters into crisis? Take a vacation in another country.

242. My president said he would protect families. That's why they lock them in their homes with curfews.

243. What do banks and mobsters have in common? Both offer you help, but always with interest.

244. In my country, elections are like exams: everyone cheats, but the results are already decided.

245. What does a corrupt judge do when he retires? He writes a book entitled "How to be fair without being fair."

246. My neighbor wanted to be a deputy. Now he has a salary he never imagined... and we have more taxes.

247. Why do politicians love social media? Because it allows them to lie to more people in less time.

248. In my country, the only reform that is moving forward is that of the prices of thebasic basket.

249. What does a bank do when you collect your salary? He sends you a letter to remind you how much you owe them.

250. My president promised to fight climate change. Now his private plane has solar panels... but it still uses fossil fuel.

250 Very Black and Cruel Humor Jokes about Death

1-50

1. What is a corpse doing in an amusement park?
   Practice freefall… forever.

2. My grandfather always said, "When I die, I want to go to heaven."
   We buried him on the highest hill to save him the trip.

3. Why don't ghosts pay taxes?
   Because they already gave everything they had in life.

4. My neighbor died doing what he loved most:
   Losing risky bets.

5. What did the coffin say to the corpse?
   "This will be more comfortable than your bed."

6. Why are cemeteries never empty?
   Because the place is always dead.

7. My friend asked me to cremate him if anything happened to him.
   Now he is the spark of all our conversations.

8. What is a ghost doing at a funeral?
   Evaluate who deserves to be scared next.

9. Why don't the dead need health insurance?
   Because the bills no longer haunt them.

10. My grandfather wanted to be remembered as a hero.
    That's why we put a cape in his coffin.

11. What did the tombstone say to the new corpse?
    "I hope you like the shade."

12. What is a corpse doing at a wedding?
    Confirms that "until death do us part" works.

13. My neighbor always said he hated commitments.
    He is now tied to a coffin.

14. Why don't the dead wear shoes?
Because no one sees your style in the cemetery.

15. What is a skeleton doing at a party?
Break the ice... literally.

16. My cousin wanted to plan his funeral in advance.
Now his will includes live music and a DJ.

17. What did the dead man say to the gravedigger?
"Dig deep, because I don't want to go back."

18. Why do the dead never complain about the weather?
Because they are already used to the cold.

19. My grandfather said he wanted to "go Viking style."
So we burned it with his couch.

20. What is a corpse doing in a morgue?
He's looking forward to his big debut on CSI.

21. What did the ghost say to the priest?
"Don't bother, I already like this place."

22. My neighbor always said that life was a joke.
Now his tombstone has the punchline.

23. Why do the dead never arrive late?
Because they are already where they should be.

24. My friend asked to be cremated.
It's now lighter than ever.

25. What's a skeleton doing in the closet?
Wait until Halloween to go out.

26. My grandfather always said he wanted to rest in peace.
So we buried him with pillows.

27. What did the earth say to the corpse?
"Welcome to your new home."

28. Why don't ghosts wear hats?

Because they always fall.

29. My neighbor wanted to save on his funeral.
    That's why they buried him in the back garden.

30. What is a corpse doing in a swimming pool?
    He floats as if he has no worries.

31. My cousin wanted a themed funeral.
    Now his coffin has wheels and a Formula 1 design.

32. What did the coffin say to the cemetery?
    "Thanks for the space."

33. Why don't the dead celebrate birthdays?
    Because the years no longer count.

34. My grandfather wanted to be cremated, but we didn't have the budget.
    So we left it in the sun.

35. What is a corpse doing in a parade?
    He makes sure not to steal the spotlight.

36. What did the tombstone say to the dead man?
    "Don't worry, nobody bothers you here."

37. My friend wanted to be useful after death.
    Now your body is an excellent fertilizer.

38. Why do the dead never fight?
    Because they have nothing to gain.

39. My grandfather asked to be buried with his watch.
    Now we know exactly how long he's been dead.

40. What is a dead body doing on a boat?
    Take part in a "ghost pirates" reenactment.

41. Why don't ghosts need to eat?
    Because they are already full of regrets.

42. My neighbor wanted to be an icon after his death.

That's why his tombstone has LED lights.

43. What did the coffin say to the dead man inside?
"I promise not to let you fall."

44. Why don't dead people use cell phones?
Because they have no one to call.

45. My cousin always said he wanted to be ashes.
It is now spread across four continents.

46. What is a skeleton doing in an anatomy class?
It becomes the perfect model.

47. Why are cemeteries so quiet?
Because nobody is in a hurry.

48. My grandfather wanted a funeral in style.
Now his coffin has a sunroof.

49. What did the dead man say to the doctor who treated him?
"Thank you for your effort, even though you arrived late."

50. Why do the dead never ask for money back?
Because the place where they are has no guarantee.

Very Black Humor and Cruel Humor Jokes about Death (51-100)

51. What is a corpse doing in a costume shop?
Wait for someone to mistake you for a mannequin.

52. My grandfather always said that life was short.
That's why he never bothered to buy a watch.

53. Why don't dead people go to the gym?
Because they are already at their ideal weight... dead.

54. What did the coffin say to the cemetery?
"I brought another well-sealed package."

55. My neighbor wanted to save on his funeral.
It is now buried in a recycled wooden box.

56. Why don't ghosts need wallets?
    Because they have nothing left to lose.

57. My cousin asked for his coffin to have wheels.
    Now we carry it around like it's a suitcase at the airport.

58. What is a corpse doing in a morgue?
    Waiting for your turn to be the center of attention.

59. What did the earth say to the newly buried corpse?
    "Welcome, neighbor!"

60. My grandfather wanted to be remembered as a strong man.
    That's why his tombstone weighs more than a car.

61. Why do the dead never visit the living?
    Because there is no GPS signal in the afterlife.

62. What is a skeleton doing in a restaurant?
    Ask for baked bones.

63. My friend asked for his funeral to be "joyful."
    So we hired a mariachi group to play at the cemetery.

64. What did the coffin say to the dead man?
    "This is the most comfortable you will ever be for the rest of your life."

65. Why don't ghosts need light?
    Because they are always illuminated... by horror.

66. My neighbor wanted to be "natural" even after death.
    That's why they buried him without a coffin.

67. What is a corpse doing at a wedding?
    It confirms that marriage isn't always the worst idea.

68. What did the tombstone say to the dead man?
    "I will take care of your legacy, even if no one else does."

69. My grandfather asked to be cremated along with his hat.
    Now his ashes are always well dressed.

70. Why do cemeteries have visiting hours?
Because the dead also need rest.

71. My cousin wanted a cheap funeral.
It now rests in a reinforced cardboard box.

72. What is a corpse doing in a hospital?
Wait for him to be discharged... forever.

73. What did the coffin say to the new tenant?
"I hope you don't snore."

74. Why don't ghosts have social media?
Because they already have enough drama in the afterlife.

75. My grandfather always said he wanted to leave in style.
That's why her coffin is encrusted with crystals.

76. What is a skeleton doing on a dance floor?
It makes sure not to break in the process.

77. Why don't the dead celebrate Christmas?
Because they have no presents to open.

78. My neighbor wanted to save on funeral expenses.
Now he was buried in the same suit he wore at his wedding.

79. What did the coffin say to the cemetery?
"Always full, never empty."

80. Why don't ghosts need vacations?
Because they are already in eternal rest.

81. My cousin requested that his tombstone have LED lights.
Now it lights up the cemetery every night.

82. What is a corpse doing in an antique shop?
It blends perfectly with the relics.

83. What did the earth say to the corpse?
"I hope you like composting."

84. My grandfather wanted his tombstone to have a memorable

phrase.
Now he says: "I finally have peace... and personal space."

85. Why don't the dead need music?
Because they already have absolute silence.

86. My neighbor wanted a modern funeral.
Now your coffin has Wi-Fi connection.

87. What is a corpse doing in a parade?
He is the only person who does not move.

88. What did the coffin say to the dead man?
"Don't worry, I have everything under control."

89. Why don't ghosts wear watches?
Because time no longer means anything to them.

90. My friend asked that his ashes be scattered at sea.
It is now part of a reef that no fish visit.

91. What is a skeleton doing in a clothing store?
Try to find something that fits snugly.

92. Why don't dead people have pets?
Because nobody wants to take care of a ghost.

93. My grandfather always said that humor is eternal.
That's why his epitaph has a QR code with his best jokes.

94. What is a dead body doing in a mattress store?
Test which one is more comfortable for "eternal rest".

95. What did the tombstone say to the newly deceased?
"I hope you settle in quickly."

96. Why don't ghosts need keys?
Because they always go through the doors.

97. My cousin wanted to be unique even in death.
That's why his coffin is painted like a racing car.

98. What is a dead body doing in a water park?

He waits patiently at the bottom of the pool.

99. What did the coffin say to the gravedigger?
"Hard work, but someone has to do it."

100. Why don't ghosts play hide and seek?
Because they always give themselves away with their sighs.

Very Black Humor and Cruel Humor Jokes about Death (101-150)

101. What is a corpse doing in a car cemetery?
Feels like home, among forgotten junk.

102. My grandfather asked to be buried with his bicycle.
He is now the only cyclist with "eternal assistance".

103. Why don't ghosts need mirrors?
Because they always see through them.

104. My neighbor wanted to save on his funeral.
That's why they buried him in a plywood coffin.

105. What did the tombstone say to the dead man?
"I hope you're not claustrophobic."

106. Why don't the dead have debts?
Because they can't sign new contracts.

107. My cousin asked for his funeral to be "different."
That's why they buried him with a band playing cumbia.

108. What is a skeleton doing in an anatomy class?
He becomes the "best student" without saying a word.

109. What did the coffin say to the new corpse?
"This will be a forever relationship."

110. Why do cemeteries have so many flowers?
Because the dead like to decorate their eternal rest.

111. My grandfather always said that he hated long procedures.
That's why we incinerate it directly.

112.What is a corpse doing in a bookstore?
It becomes an "open book" for forensic experts.

113.Why don't ghosts wear shoes?
Because they always lose the sole.

114.My neighbor wanted his tombstone to have modern technology.
Now it has a fingerprint reader... that nobody uses.

115.What did the earth say to the corpse?
"See you for a long time."

116.Why do the dead never have holidays?
Because they are already in their eternal rest.

117.My friend requested that his tombstone be interactive.
Now you can play "Tetris" while you visit.

118.What is a corpse doing in a swimming pool?
It becomes the most disturbing float.

119.What did the coffin say to the gravedigger?
"Thank you for the profound journey."

120.Why don't ghosts play sports?
Because they are always out of shape.

121.My cousin wanted his funeral to be unique.
That's why his coffin had neon lights.

122.What is a corpse doing in a zoo?
It becomes the most "natural" attraction.

123.What did the tombstone say to the newly deceased?
"Welcome to the club of the immobile."

124.Why do the dead never arrive late?
Because they have nowhere to go.

125.My grandfather asked to be buried with his television.
Now he enjoys his favorite shows... in the afterlife.

126.What is a corpse doing at a fashion show?

Makes sure that black is always in fashion.

127. What did the coffin say to the cemetery?
"This is my new VIP client."

128. Why don't ghosts have children?
Because nobody wants to inherit their emptiness.

129. My neighbor wanted a minimalist funeral.
That's why they buried him with nothing... except his body.

130. What is a corpse doing in a cooking class?
Wait until it becomes the main ingredient in a horror story.

131. What did the tombstone say to the dead man?
"I hope you enjoy the view."

132. Why don't dead people use umbrellas?
Because they never mind getting wet.

133. My cousin always said that he loved the sea.
That's why his ashes were scattered in the ocean... along with a bottle of rum.

134. What is a corpse doing in a theater?
Steals the show without saying a word.

135. What did the coffin say to the new corpse?
"I hope you're not afraid of the dark."

136. Why don't ghosts need to eat?
Because they live off the memories of the living.

137. My grandfather asked for his coffin to have windows.
Now he has the best "apartment" in the cemetery.

138. What is a dead body doing in a furniture store?
Expect to be mistaken for a sculpture.

139. What did the earth say to the newly arrived corpse?
"I hope you feel well grounded."

140. Why don't the dead use technology?

Because they never update their software.

141. My neighbor wanted to save on funeral expenses.
That's why they buried him in his favorite pajamas.

142. What is a corpse doing in a play?
Makes sure the drama is real.

143. What did the coffin say to the dead man?
"Welcome to your final resting place."

144. Why don't ghosts need clocks?
Because they already live in eternal time.

145. My friend wanted to be unique at his funeral.
That's why his coffin is painted like a gift box.

146. What is a corpse doing in a bookstore?
Wait for someone to write their story.

147. What did the tombstone say to the new corpse?
"Don't worry, everything is quiet here."

148. Why don't the dead celebrate anniversaries?
Because they have nothing to celebrate anymore.

149. My grandfather always said he wanted a fun farewell.
That's why we hired a comedian for his funeral.

150. What is a corpse doing at a costume party?
He is mistaken for the winner of the best costume.

Very Black Humor and Cruel Humor Jokes about Death (151-200)

151. What is a corpse doing in a museum?
Wait to be labeled as "modern art."

152. My grandfather wanted his epitaph to be unique.
Now he says: "Here I am, but I prefer not to be."

153. Why don't ghosts have beds?
Because they are always standing... even if they don't have feet.

154. My cousin requested that his coffin have music built into it.
Now relax in rhythm with your favorite playlist.

155. What is a corpse doing in a chemistry class?
Wait until it's the final project.

156. What did the tombstone say to the corpse?
"I hope you get settled quickly, this place is packed."

157. Why don't dead people have pets?
Because they can't even take care of themselves.

158. My neighbor wanted his tombstone to be interactive.
Now plays automatic messages when someone passes by.

159. What is a dead body doing in an electronics store?
He searches for his last connection to the world.

160. What did the coffin say to the gravedigger?
"Don't forget that I'm heavy, literally."

161. Why don't ghosts need heating?
Because they are already accustomed to the cold of eternity.

162. My grandfather wanted a funeral full of technology.
That's why you can now watch it streaming from his grave.

163. What is a corpse doing at a rock concert?
He's the only one who doesn't scream, but he's still the palest.

164. What did the tombstone say to the newly arrived dead man?
"Relax, there's no traffic here."

165. Why don't the dead play chess?
Because they always end up in a draw.

166. My friend wanted to be cremated in his favorite bar.
Now it is the spark of every meeting.

167. What is a corpse doing in a play?
He waits for someone to applaud him... even though he will never hear it.

168.What did the coffin say to the cemetery?
   "One more for the collection."

169.Why don't ghosts need umbrellas?
   Because they are already used to getting wet with tears.

170.My cousin wanted to save on his funeral.
   That's why they buried him in a folding coffin.

171.What is a corpse doing in a supermarket?
   Wait for someone to mistake this for a Halloween promotion.

172.What did the tombstone say to the dead man?
   "Don't worry, I will carry the weight of your legacy."

173.Why don't the dead need schedules?
   Because they are no longer in a hurry.

174.My grandfather asked to be buried with his dog.
   The dog was not so happy with the idea.

175.What is a corpse doing in an art gallery?
   Wait for someone to consider it a valuable piece.

176.What did the coffin say to the dead man?
   "I hope you are comfortable, because there are no refunds."

177.Why don't ghosts go to the gym?
   Because they are always out of shape... literally.

178.My friend wanted his tombstone to be fun.
   Now he says: "I rest here, but I hate getting up early."

179.What is a corpse doing in a candle factory?
   Wait for them to use it as inspiration.

180.What did the tombstone say to the newly deceased?
   "You came just in time for eternal silence!"

181.Why don't the dead need shoes?
   Because they will never take another step.

182.My neighbor wanted a unique funeral.

That's why they buried him with a light show and fireworks.

183. What is a corpse doing in a costume shop?
It makes sure to be the most realistic on Halloween.

184. What did the coffin say to the gravedigger?
"Thank you for the profound journey."

185. Why don't ghosts need food?
Because they are already full of regrets.

186. My grandfather wanted his coffin to be recyclable.
That's why it's now a table in his family's living room.

187. What is a corpse doing in a morgue?
He waits patiently for his turn in the afterlife.

188. What did the tombstone say to the new corpse?
"Don't worry, there's never any noise here."

189. Why don't the dead celebrate anniversaries?
Because every day is the same for them.

190. My friend wanted his coffin to be modern.
That's why he has a solar panel to charge his electronic tombstone.

191. What is a corpse doing in a parade?
It's the only one that doesn't move, but it attracts attention.

192. What did the coffin say to the dead man?
"This will be the most lasting experience of your life."

193. Why don't ghosts have friends?
Because they are always passing through.

194. My cousin asked for his tombstone to be "innovative."
Now he broadcasts his epitaph in holograms.

195. What is a corpse doing in a literature class?
Wait until you're the main character in a horror story.

196. What did the tombstone say to the newly deceased?

"I hope you enjoy the eternal silence."

197.Why don't the dead need vacations?
Because they are already in their final rest.

198.My grandfather wanted to be remembered as a practical man.
That's why his coffin also functions as a piece of furniture.

199.What is a corpse doing in a swimming pool?
Expect to be mistaken for a practice dummy.

200.What did the coffin say to the cemetery?
"I bring a new tenant to your neighborhood."

Very Black Humor and Cruel Humor Jokes about Death (201-250)

201.What is a corpse doing in an antique shop?
Wait until they label it a "historical relic."

202.My grandfather asked to be buried with his favorite watch.
Now he always arrives punctually to the eternal silence.

203.Why don't ghosts go sightseeing?
Because they have seen it all... from beyond.

204.My cousin wanted his funeral to be unforgettable.
That's why we hired a magician who made his coffin disappear right in the middle of the act.

205.What is a corpse doing in a gym?
It gives the living a lesson in what it means to "rest forever."

206.What did the tombstone say to the newly arrived dead man?
"Welcome to the club of the immobile."

207.Why don't the dead need cell phones?
Because they are already out of coverage.

208.My neighbor wanted to save on his funeral.
That's why his tombstone is a brick painted with his name.

209.What is a corpse doing in a theme park?
It's the only attraction that never screams.

210. What did the coffin say to the cemetery?
"Thank you for always making a place for me."

211. Why don't ghosts need to work?
Because they are already out of the labor market.

212. My grandfather always said he wanted "a brilliant ending."
That's why we filled her urn with glitter.

213. What is a dead body doing in a jewelry store?
Wait for it to be used as a macabre display.

214. What did the tombstone say to the dead man?
"Don't worry, I'll carry your story."

215. Why don't the dead exercise?
Because they are already in their best form... skeletal.

216. My friend asked that his epitaph be funny.
Now he says: "I rest here, but if something wakes me up, run."

217. What is a corpse doing in a science class?
It becomes the perfect example for "advanced decomposition".

218. What did the coffin say to the gravedigger?
"I always deliver my packages on time."

219. Why don't ghosts need clothes?
Because nobody notices if they are naked.

220. My cousin wanted his tombstone to be state-of-the-art.
Now your epitaph is automatically updated with the newslocal.

221. What is a corpse doing in a supermarket?
He becomes the special guest of the Halloween section.

222. What did the tombstone say to the newly deceased?
"I hope you don't mind the visitors."

223. Why don't the dead write autobiographies?
Because their history is already engraved... in stone.

224. My grandfather wanted a themed funeral.

That's why they buried him in a pirate costume.

225.What is a corpse doing in a bookstore?
Wait for someone to mistake this for a 3D horror book.

226.What did the coffin say to the dead man?
"I promise to be your most enduring refuge."

227.Why don't ghosts wear watches?
Because they always live in the moment.

228.My neighbor wanted to be "different" even in death.
That's why his tombstone is shaped like a giant diamond.

229.What is a corpse doing in a math class?
Wait until you are the perfect example of "definitive subtractions."

230.What did the tombstone say to the newly arrived dead man?
"Relax, no one is rushing you here."

231.Why don't the dead need to learn languages?
Because silence is universal.

232.My grandfather wanted his coffin to have wheels.
Now we push it like a shopping cart.

233.What is a corpse doing in a parade?
He makes sure everyone sees what it means to "be at the bottom."

234.What did the coffin say to the cemetery?
"I always deliver my content intact."

235.Why don't ghosts go to the doctor?
Because there is nothing left to lose.

236.My cousin wanted his tombstone to have colors.
Now it looks like a piece of pop art in the middle of the cemetery.

237.What is a corpse doing in a toy store?
It becomes the favorite of the scare section.

238. What did the tombstone say to the newly deceased?
"I hope you settle in quickly; this neighborhood is very quiet."

239. Why don't the dead need friends?
Because they are already in the company of their own thoughts... eternal.

240. My grandfather asked that his epitaph be practical.
Now he says, "There's room for one more person here."

241. What is a dead body doing in a public pool?
He confuses everyone with his "still swimming style".

242. What did the coffin say to the gravedigger?
"Don't forget to press the earth; I like to feel safe."

243. Why don't ghosts get married?
Because nobody wants a love that haunts you forever.

244. My neighbor wanted his coffin to be innovative.
That's why it now has ventilation... just in case.

245. What is a dead body doing in a shopping mall?
Wait patiently to be the scariest mannequin.

246. What did the tombstone say to the dead man?
"Relax, no one here speaks ill of you... yet."

247. Why don't the dead have parties?
Because they are always the missing soul.

248. My grandfather asked to be buried with his radio.
Now tune in to the stations of the beyond.

249. What is a corpse doing in a Halloween parade?
He makes sure that no one mistakes him for a cheap costume.

250. What did the coffin say to the cemetery?
"Always full, never empty."

CLOWN DOWN

250 Very Dark and Cruel Jokes from Everyday Life

1-50

1. Why do accounts never cry?
   Because they already have the humans to do it.

2. My friend bought a sofa so comfortable he never got up from it again... literally.

3. What did the alarm clock say to its owner?
   "Get up, for a happy sleep is for the dead."

4. Why does the microwave always make noise?
   Because it's cooking up your dreams of a better life.

5. My neighbor always said, "Today will be a great day."
   It's a pity that day never came.

6. What does a mother with three jobs do when she gets home?
   He looks at his children and says: "Be thankful that I am still here."

7. Why does the washing machine always spin?
   Because he's trying to get away from your dirty laundry.

8. My cousin quit his job to "find himself."
   We now find him living in his parents' basement.

9. What does a millennial do when he sees his debts?
   He sighs and laughs, because crying doesn't help anymore.

10. Why don't automatic doors have friends?
    Because they always open and close at the wrong time.

11. My friend asked for a vacation to relax.
    He ended up more tired than before because he couldn't stop thinking about his boss.

12. What does the iron say to wrinkled clothes?
    "At least you can hide your problems."

13. Why are Mondays so cruel?
    Because they are proof that the weekend was a lie.

14. My neighbor bought a bike for exercise.
    Now it is parked... like its goals.

15. What does an adult do with his first paycheck?
    Discover that being poor is an endless cycle.

16. Why do toasters always burn bread?
    Because they want to show you what it feels like to live in constant stress.

17. My friend bought an expensive watch.
    Now he arrives on time... to the bank to ask for another loan.

18. What does a student do after finishing university?
    Discover that having a degree doesn't pay the rent.

19. Why are refrigerators always full of air?
    Because your dreams of eating something decent vanish with every purchase.

20. My cousin bought a self-help book.
    Now he is so helped that he does nothing.

21. What does an adult do when he receives his electric bill?
    He turns everything off and wonders why he is still alive.

22. Why do cars always break down at the worst times?
    Because they want to be the priority of your despair.

23. My grandfather bought a modern cell phone.
    Now he uses it as a paperweight because he never figured out how to turn it on.

24. What does a child do with an expensive toy?
    He breaks it in less time than it took you to pay for it.

25. Why do vacuum cleaners make so much noise?
    Because they want to show that they work harder than you.

26. My neighbor wanted to save water.
    Now your garden looks like the Sahara Desert.

27. What did the scale tell its owner?
"Your relationship with me is pure emotional weight."

28. Why do headphones always get tangled?
Because even they hate being in your pocket.

29. My friend wanted to get rich by investing in cryptocurrencies.
Now he spends his time looking for a job.

30. What does a mother do when her child says "I can't take it anymore"?
He answers: "Me neither, but we are still here."

31. Why do fans always spin so fast?
Because they are trying to escape the heat of your problems.

32. My cousin bought a planner to be organized.
Now you have everything written down except how to achieve it.

33. What is an empty fridge doing in the middle of a crisis?
It reminds you that you are alone in this world.

34. Why are desk lamps so bright?
To illuminate the darkness of your failures.

35. My friend wanted to be an influencer.
Now it influences... no one.

36. What does a mirror say to someone who is depressed?
"At least you have the nerve to show it."

37. Why do phones always run out of battery in emergencies?
Because they like to dramatize your life.

38. My neighbor bought a treadmill.
Now she uses it to hang clothes.

39. What does an ATM do when you have no money?
It shows you your negative balance with a virtual smile.

40. Why do washing machines eat socks?
Because they want to show that your life is a mess.

41. My cousin started a diet.
    It lasted less than his last attempt to pay off debts.

42. What does the wifi tell the user when it is not working?
    "I have bad days too."

43. Why do alarms always sound so loud?
    Because they want to remind you that you have no escape.

44. My friend bought a new coffee maker.
    Now he has coffee, but he still has no energy to live.

45. What does a TV do when it's off?
    It reflects your tired face.

46. Why are dogs so happy?
    Because they don't have to pay rent.

47. My neighbor wanted to be a minimalist.
    Now he lives with less things... and less happiness.

48. What does a cat do when you ignore it?
    He'd rather ignore you.

49. Why do the bills all arrive together?
    Because they like to team up to ruin your day.

50. My grandfather bought a hammock to relax in.
    Now the hammock has more movement than him.

Continuation: Very Black and Cruel Jokes of Daily Life (51-100)

51. What is a coffee maker doing in a house without coffee?
    He laughs at your attempts to start the day.

52. My neighbor bought a stationary bike for training.
    Now it sits there, collecting dust.

53. Why do white shirts always get stained on the first day?
    Because they know that chaos is inevitable.

54. What is a to-do list doing on your desk?
    He watches you while you do everything except what you wrote

down.

55. My friend wanted to do meditation to relax.
Now he's just thinking about how to pay his bills.

56. Why do candles go out quickly?
Because they don't want to be in your life any longer than necessary.

57. What does an adult do when he or she receives a "special offers" email?
Ignore it, because you know you can't buy anything.

58. My cousin wanted to learn yoga to improve his life.
Now he can double his income, but he still can't make ends meet.

59. Why do cell phone chargers always disappear?
Because they prefer to hide rather than continue to put up with your carelessness.

60. What is a robot vacuum cleaner doing in a house with children?
He quietly resigns.

61. My neighbor bought an electric car to save gas.
Now he spends more on his electricity bill.

62. Why are the mirrors in elevators always so clean?
So you can see your desperate face as you walk up to the office.

63. What does a printer do when you need something urgently?
He decides that it's the perfect time to get stuck.

64. My friend wanted to be "eco-friendly".
Now recycle more excuses than plastic.

65. Why do scales always indicate more than you expect?
Because they know you can't deal with the truth.

66. What does an adult do when they receive a "payment reminder" email?
He sighs, ignores the message and prepares for another fine.

67. My cousin bought an ergonomic chair to work from home.
Now he only uses it to sleep better while sitting up.

68. Why do fast chargers never charge fast when you need them most?
Because they have their own rhythm of life.

69. What does a clock do when you have no time for anything?
It reminds you that it is always moving forward, even if you are not.

70. My grandfather bought an air conditioner to enjoy the summer.
Now he struggles with the electricity bill every month.

71. Why do new shoes always hurt?
Because they want to remind you that nothing good in life is free.

72. What does an adult do when he receives an "urgent package"?
She wonders why he always comes home when she's not at home.

73. My friend wanted to learn how to cook to save money.
Now he spends more on gourmet recipes than on fast food.

74. Why are wall clocks always so loud in the middle of the night?
Because they know you can't sleep, so they keep you company.

75. What does an appliance do when its warranty ends?
It stops working at the most inconvenient moment.

76. My neighbor wanted to redecorate his house.
He now lives in a modern ruin he calls "minimalism."

77. Why do phones never have enough space?
Because they prefer to store your photographic mistakes rather than happy memories.

78. What does an adult do when he receives a message from his bank?
You feel a little heart attack, even if it's just a promotion announcement.

79. My cousin wanted to be a vegetarian to feel better.

Now he eats grass, but he still feels empty inside.

80. Why do water bottles always fall at the worst times?
Because they are tired of being ignored.

81. What does a lamp do when the bulb burns out?
It leaves you in the dark, to reflect on your decisions.

82. My friend bought a safe to "protect his savings."
Now the till is fuller than your bank account.

83. Why do closet doors always creak at night?
Because they like to add drama to your insomnia.

84. What does a microwave do when it finishes heating?
He whistles like he just saved the world.

85. My neighbor bought a smart coffee maker.
Now he has coffee, but he still lacks emotional intelligence.

86. Why are pillows never as comfortable as they are in the store?
Because at home they know that your dreams are impossible.

87. What does an adult do when he sees his credit card bill?
He promises he will never spend again... until his next purchase.

88. My friend wanted to be a "minimalist."
Now he lives with fewer things, but more frustration.

89. Why do self-help books always seem so easy to read?
Because they know you will never apply them.

90. What does a fan do when it's extremely hot?
It spins faster, but it still doesn't solve your problems.

91. My cousin wanted to open his own business.
Now his business has him locked into eternal debt.

92. Why do phone cameras always fail at important moments?
Because they like to watch you miss the opportunity of a lifetime.

93. What does a rechargeable battery do when you need it most?
He decides he doesn't want to burden himself anymore.

94. My grandfather bought a state-of-the-art watch.
Now you know the exact time when everything is still just as boring.

95. Why do long voicemails always come when you're busy?
Because they want to remind you that no one respects your time.

96. What does an adult do when he sees his food burning in the oven?
Consider ordering delivery while the disaster continues to occur.

97. My friend wanted to go to the gym to change his life.
Now his life has changed: he is more tired, but just as fat.

98. Why do remotes always get lost?
Because they need their own time away from your dramas.

99. What does an adult do when he sees an "irresistible" offer?
Buy something you'll never use, but at a huge discount.

100. My neighbor wanted to be the master of his own destiny.
Now his destiny leads him directly to unemployment.

Very Dark and Cruel Jokes from Everyday Life (101-150)

101. Why do invoice envelopes always open by themselves?
Because they can't wait to ruin your day.

102. My friend bought a plant to "de-stress."
Now he is more stressed because the plant is dying.

103. What does a frying pan do when you burn food?
It reminds you that cooking was not your talent.

104. Why do alarm clocks always go off at the best time of night?
Because they hate seeing you happy, even when you're asleep.

105. My neighbor bought a sports car to impress.
Now he impresses debt collectors more than his friends.

106. What does an adult do when his salary is not enough?
He consoles himself by thinking that "at least he is alive"... although he doesn't know for how long.

107. Why do washing machines always fail with the most expensive clothes?
Because they want to teach you a lesson about your priorities.

108. My cousin wanted to adopt a healthy lifestyle.
Now he lives longer... but without enjoying anything.

109. What does an adult do when he runs out of toilet paper?
He thinks it's the perfect summary of his life: being left with nothing at the worst time.

110. Why do grocery bags always break?
Because they don't want to carry your problems.

111. My friend bought an expensive mattress to sleep better.
He sleeps better now, but wakes up crying over the debt.

112. What does a coffee maker do when it has no coffee?
She looks at you with disappointment, just like you look at her.

113. Why do elevators always take longer when you're in a hurry?
Because they enjoy seeing you suffer in the little moments.

114. My neighbor wanted to learn to play the guitar to "connect with the music."
Now he is disconnected... from the rest of the world because nobody can stand him.

115. What does an adult do when they run out of mobile data?
He feels more lost than his purpose in life.

116. Why do office chairs always break when you need them?
Because they are designed to fail with you.

117. My grandfather bought a flashlight for emergencies.
The emergency came... and the flashlight didn't work.

118. What does an adult do when he forgets his password?
Create a new one, which you will also forget next week.

119. Why do wireless headphones always drain at the worst times?
Because they don't want to hear your problems any more than

you do.

120.My cousin wanted to start saving money.
Now he saves every penny, but he doesn't know what to spend it on because everything is expensive.

121.What does an adult do when he sees that his shoes are torn?
He still uses them because buying new ones is not in the budget.

122.Why do windows always get broken by balls?
Because they want to remind you that the game and life are never fair.

123.My friend wanted to become a chef.
Now she cooks her tears because no one pays for her food.

124.What does a flickering light bulb do?
It shows you what your life is like: brilliant at times, but unstable.

125.Why do ceiling fans always make noise?
Because they want you to never forget that they are there, like your problems.

126.My neighbor bought a grill to invite everyone.
Now he uses the grill as a decoration because no one brings food.

127.What does an adult do when he finds a coin on the street?
He picks it up as if it were a miracle.

128.Why do digital clocks always reset themselves?
Because they want you to never trust them...or anything else.

129.My cousin wanted to be a graphic designer.
Now he designs "Room for rent" signs.

130.What does an adult do when his car won't start?
Think how easy it would be to disappear with him.

131.Why do ovens always burn your important meals?
Because they know that romantic dinners will never be perfect.

132.My friend wanted to start exercising.

Now he does this: he walks to save on transportation.

133. What does a computer do when you forget to save your work?
It turns off, because it enjoys your suffering.

134. Why do doors creak more at night?
Because they want to participate in your dark thoughts.

135. My neighbor bought a state-of-the-art coffee maker.
Now his life is just as bitter, but with a better aroma.

136. What does an adult do when he sees that there is no food at home?
He goes to sleep early, because dreaming is free.

137. Why do bathroom lights always burn out first?
Because they know that this is where you spend your best time reflecting.

138. My cousin wanted to start his own business.
Now he is the owner... of a very large debt.

139. What does an adult do when a "special offers" email arrives?
He ignores the offer, because he can't afford it even with a discount.

140. Why do blinds always break when you try to open them?
Because they like to keep you in the dark, like your financial life.

141. My friend bought a planner to "get better organized."
Now you have an organized list of things you will never do.

142. What does an adult do when he receives a call from an unknown number?
He assumes it's the bank and panics.

143. Why do cars always run out of gas on the road?
Because they want to be the center of your despair.

144. My neighbor wanted to save energy by turning off the lights.
Now he lives in the shadows, just like his expectations.

145. What does an adult do when he loses his keys?
He begins to philosophize about what he has lost in life.

146. Why do cell phone chargers always fail on one side?
Because they enjoy complicating the simplest things for you.

147. My cousin wanted to dedicate himself to art.
Now his art is selling drawings at fairs for two coins.

148. What does an adult do when he runs out of money in the middle of the month?
Practice the noble art of surviving with air and hope.

149. Why do used cars always break down right after you buy them?
Because they want to show you that life is always a gamble.

150. My grandfather bought an armchair to relax in.
Now it is the place where he spends 90% of his life watching soap operas.

Very Dark and Cruel Jokes from Everyday Life (151-200)

151. What does an adult do when checking his bank balance?
Look at the screen as if it were a horror movie.

152. My neighbor bought a zen garden to relax.
Now he is more stressed because he can never rake it perfectly.

153. Why do light bulbs always burn out when you need them the most?
Because they want you to get used to the darkness.

154. My friend wanted to be an entrepreneur.
Now he sells his things to pay off his business debts.

155. What does an adult do when his cell phone falls to the floor?
He prays as if that would save his wallet.

156. Why do new jackets always lose buttons?
Because nothing in life can remain complete.

157. My cousin wanted to learn to play the piano to impress.

Now it just impresses the neighbors with the constant noise.

158. What does a bicycle do when it sees you coming?
He prepares his chains to get stuck at the most painful moment.

159. Why are buses always late when you are in a hurry?
Because they know that nothing in your life is punctual.

160. My grandfather bought a rocking chair to relax in.
Now he only uses it to sleep thinking about his regrets.

161. What does a printer do when you have an important exam?
Decide to take a vacation.

162. Why do headphones always stop working on one side?
Because they want you to get used to hearing less.

163. My neighbor wanted to adopt a dog to feel accompanied.
Now he has a furry friend... and a house full of hair.

164. What does a TV do when the power goes out?
It reminds you that not everything depends on you, except your frustration.

165. Why do coins always fall under furniture?
Because they prefer to hide from your economic desperation.

166. My cousin wanted to be "sustainable".
He now lives without electricity and feels more miserable than ecological.

167. What does an adult do when he hears a notification on his cell phone?
Hopefully it's not just another bill.

168. Why do garbage bags always tear when you take them out?
Because they want you to face your waste like in real life.

169. My friend bought a new blender to improve his diet.
Now he's blending everything... except his love life.

170. What does a bed do when you decide to get up early?

He invites you back, because he knows you can't resist.

171.Why do glasses always get lost when you need them the most?
Because they like to play hide and seek with your patience.

172.My neighbor bought a smart air conditioner.
Now he is fresh, but with a debt that suffocates him.

173.What does an adult do when he receives a call from the bank?
He prepares for a "I have no money" speech.

174.Why do umbrellas always disappear when it rains?
Because they want you to learn how to deal with wet chaos.

175.My cousin wanted to start running every day.
Now run... to catch the bus.

176.What does a coffee maker do when it runs out of coffee?
It leaves you without hope or motivation.

177.Why do computers always update at the most inopportune
times?
Because they want to remind you that you will never be in control.

178.My grandfather wanted to be modern and buy a tablet.
Now she uses it as a coffee tray.

179.What does an adult do when he loses his credit card?
He feels relieved until he remembers that he needs to report her.

180.Why do brushes always lose bristles so quickly?
Because they know you already have enough things to fix in life.

181.My friend wanted to learn to paint to relax.
Now he paints his frustration because it never turns out right.

182.What does a window do when you close it carefully?
It breaks, because it doesn't like to be treated gently.

183.Why do car lights always fail at night?
Because they like to add drama to your road problems.

184.My neighbor bought an exercise machine to get in shape.

It is now in the form of a coat rack.

185. What does an adult do when the weekend comes?
He realizes that he also has to work on Monday.

186. Why do bananas always ripen when you don't need them?
Because they want to be a reflection of your late decisions.

187. My cousin wanted to learn programming to earn more money.
Now he earns less because he spends all day learning.

188. What does a microwave do when it doesn't heat properly?
It teaches you that fast things are never perfect.

189. Why do keys always disappear at the most inconvenient times?
Because they like to see you lose control.

190. My grandfather bought a fancy wristwatch.
Now he uses it to count the minutes he wastes.

191. What does a stove do when you need to cook something fast?
He decides that today he is going to warm up at his own pace.

192. Why are electrical outlets always placed incorrectly?
Because they like to complicate even the simplest things.

193. My friend wanted to learn carpentry to make his own furniture.
Now he has a wobbly table and a debt to the hardware store.

194. What does an adult do when he receives a traffic ticket?
He consoles himself with the thought that at least he is alive to pay for it.

195. Why do bikes always go flat when you plan to use them?
Because they also need a break from your intentions.

196. My neighbor wanted to redecorate his house.
Now he has less money and more clutter.

197. What does an adult do when their TV stops working?
He looks at the wall and reflects on his sad existence.

198. Why do clocks always go forward when you're late?

Because they want to show that even time abandons you.

199.My cousin wanted to become a musician.
Now he plays for himself because no one listens to him.

200.What does a fan do when you need it to sleep?
It makes a noise like a plane taking off.

Very Dark and Cruel Jokes from Everyday Life (201-250)

201.Why are electrical outlets always out of reach?
Because they like to see you stretch yourself into awkward positions.

202.My neighbor bought a food processor to save time.
Now you waste more time understanding the manual.

203.What does a shower do when you need hot water?
You decide it's the perfect time to freeze.

204.Why are reusable bags always forgotten in the car?
Because they like to remind you how inefficient you are.

205.My cousin wanted to be a professional photographer.
Now you have beautiful photos... but no chance of selling them.

206.What does an adult do when he finds money in his pocket?
He feels rich... until he remembers all his debts.

207.Why do appliances always break down right after the warranty period?
Because they are programmed to betray you.

208.My friend bought a smart watch to improve his life.
Now the watch knows more about him than his therapist.

209.What does an umbrella do when it starts to rain?
It breaks, to make sure you get wet.

210.Why do your glasses always get dirty when you need to see well the most?
Because they enjoy clouding your vision, just like life.

211. My grandfather wanted to save on transportation by buying a bicycle.
Now he spends more on knee pads after every fall.

212. What does a toaster do when you're in a hurry?
He takes his time as if he were cooking a feast.

213. Why do sandals always break on the street?
Because they want to make sure you feel every step of your misfortune.

214. My neighbor wanted to fix his house himself.
Now there are more patches on the walls than happy memories.

215. What does an adult do when they receive a "payment pending" email?
He ignores it, because he knows there is no escape.

216. Why do cats always knock things off tables?
Because they want to remind you that they are in control.

217. My cousin wanted to buy designer clothes to look better.
Now it looks good, but only at events you can't afford.

218. What does a microwave do when something inside it explodes?
He looks at you like it's your fault... even though it is.

219. Why do plants always die when you take too much care of them?
Because they can't stand your control issues.

220. My friend bought an inflatable pool to relax in.
Now the pool is punctured and so is his patience.

221. What does an adult do when he runs into his ex in public?
She wonders why he's not dead... or why her ex isn't.

222. Why do cars always run out of gas on the road?
Because they like to add tension to your trips.

223. My neighbor bought a fancy coffee maker.
Now he can only drink water because he has no money for coffee.

224.What does a TV do when you change channels?
It takes him ages to respond, because he knows you're impatient.

225.Why do scissors never cut well when you need them most?
Because they enjoy ruining your projects.

226.My cousin wanted to be a writer.
Now you have a manuscript that no one wants to read.

227.What does an adult do when he loses his wallet?
Pray that at least the debts have not been lost with her.

228.Why do clocks always stop when you forget about them?
Because they want to remind you that you need constant attention, like everything in life.

229.My grandfather wanted to fix his old radio.
Now the radio is still broken... and so are his fingers.

230.What does an adult do when food burns?
He looks at the frying pan as if it were the culprit of all his problems.

231.Why do socks always disappear in the washing machine?
Because they know that alone they are worth more than together.

232.My friend wanted to learn how to paint pictures.
Now his paintings hang... in his garage.

233.What does a phone do when it runs out of battery?
He abandons you at the worst moment, just like toxic people.

234.Why do old mattresses always sag on the side you sleep on?
Because they want to remind you that you can't escape your weight... literal or emotional.

235.My neighbor bought an expensive grill to invite his friends over.
Now nobody visits him because he doesn't have money to buy meat.

236.What does a refrigerator do when it's not full?
It becomes the perfect reflection of your empty life.

237. Why do vending machines always swallow your money?
Because they want to remind you that not even they work for free.

238. My cousin wanted to start investing in the stock market.
Now he spends his time looking for ways to recover what he lost.

239. What does a fan do when you need it most?
He blows hot air at you because even he hates you.

240. Why do wireless earphones always get lost?
Because they prefer to be at the bottom of a sofa rather than in yourears.

241. My grandfather bought a hat to protect himself from the sun.
Now he uses the hat to protect his dignity while forgetting it everywhere.

242. What does an old TV do when you turn it on?
It shows you blurry lines, like your hopes.

243. Why do ATMs always run out of cash when you arrive?
Because they prefer to disappoint you face to face.

244. My friend wanted to become a model.
Now she models... for her selfies that no one sees.

245. What does a lamp do when you need light?
It burns, to make sure you stay in the dark.

246. Why do cats always sleep on your important things?
Because they know that bothers you more than anything else.

247. My neighbor wanted to be a gardener.
Now you have plants that are wilting faster than your patience.

248. What does a computer do when you need to work?
You decide it's the perfect time to upgrade.

249. Why do ceiling fans always squeak?
Because they want to be part of your nightly worries.

250.My cousin wanted to open a restaurant.

Now he cooks for no one, because the customers never came.

Reflections of the Down Clown

Acid fragments of irreverent philosophy.

1. **Life:**
   Life is like a bad joke told by someone unfunny: you laugh just to keep from crying.

2. **About death:**
   The only time you'll be truly punctual is when you get to your grave.

3. **About love:**
   Love is like a credit card: at first it seems free, but you always end up paying interest.

4. **About dreams:**
   Follow your dreams, but don't be surprised if they betray you in the end too.

5. **On hope:**
   Hope is that thin thread you use to hang your failures on.

6. **About the family:**
   Family is always there for you... especially when there is an inheritance involved.

7. **About religion:**
   If God has a plan for you, why does it always seem like the pilot episode of a failure?

8. **On success:**
   Success is nothing more than an excuse for others to hate your momentary happiness.

9. **On happiness:**
   Happiness is like socks in the washing machine: it always gets lost when you need it most.

10. **About friends:**
    Friends are the decoration you choose for your life, but some end up being as useful as a broken ornament.

11. **About money:**
    They say money can't buy happiness, but have you tried being happy while eating air?

12. **About the weather:**
    Time is that thief that steals everything from you and leaves you alone with regrets.

13. **About the future:**
    The future is that cruel joke that never quite lands.

14. **About the work:**
    You work to live, but in the end you only live to complain about work.

15. **On failure:**
    Failure is the mother of experience, but who wants to visit that mother so often?

16. **About society:**
    We live in a society where empathy is optional, but judgment is mandatory.

17. **About power:**
    Power does not corrupt; it was already corrupt when you found it.

18. **On honesty:**
    Honesty is the currency that no one wants to accept because it doesn't pay the bills.

19. **On loneliness:**
    Loneliness is like a good glass of wine: bitter at first, but you get used to it.

20. **About humanity:**
    Humanity is that failed project that continues to develop because no one wants to admit their mistake.

21.**On mental health:**

If the mind is a temple, mine must be in ruins with graffiti.

22.**About broken dreams:**

Your dreams aren't broken; they just never fit into this world.

23.**About the changes:**

Change is good, but don't forget that you can also change for the worse.

24.**About enemies:**

Your enemies are nothing more than confused admirers with an inferiority complex.

25.**About art:**

Art is the nicest way to say everything is wrong, but at least you did it with style.

26.**About silence:**

Silence is a luxury that few can afford in this noisy world.

27.**About the destination:**

Destiny doesn't exist; it's just your personal chaos disguised as a plan.

28.**About youth:**

Youth is that gift that you only value when you no longer have it.

29.**About the errors:**

Mistakes are cruel teachers who always take their toll in advance.

30.**On failure:**

Failure is not falling; failure is staying down because the ground was comfortable.

CLOWN DOWN

BONUS: 50 Extremely Strong, Cruel and Merciless Jokes

1. Why don't orphans play "Where's Mommy?"
   Because the game never ends.

2. My cousin wanted a simple funeral.
   So we left it where it fell.

3. What is a baby doing in a microwave?
   I don't know, but it's starting to smell like chicken.

4. My neighbor asked to die with dignity.
   That's why we left him in his favorite pajamas.

5. Why don't the blind argue?
   Because they don't see the point.

6. My grandfather asked to be buried with his watch.
   Now we know the exact time when nothing happens.

7. What did the parachute say to the suicide bomber?
   "I'm not working for free today."

8. Why don't the dead celebrate Christmas?
   Because they are already wrapped up all year round.

9. My friend wanted to see the world from above.
   Now his name is engraved on the pavement.

10. What is a corpse doing at a themed funeral?
    It fits perfectly with the decor.

11. Why don't zombies commit suicide?
    Because they don't have enough brains to get depressed.

12. My cousin wanted his tombstone to have a unique message.
    Now he says, "See? I told them it hurt."

13. What is a dead person doing in a yoga class?
    Practice the ultimate pose: the corpse.

14. Why don't ghosts get married?
    Because they can't find rings they can't pass through.

15. My friend wanted to die on his own terms.
    That's why he left his farewell letter in a meme.

16. What is a baby doing in a shredder?
    A guilt-ridden mash.

17. My neighbor wanted to be cremated.
    Now it's part of a barbecue that no one forgets.

18. Why do orphans hate puzzles?
    Because they always lack the main piece.

19. My cousin wanted to be immortal.
    Now it is visited by more land than people.

20. What is a dead body doing in a trash can?
    It shows that even death generates waste.

21. Why don't zombies eat in restaurants?
    Because there are no brains on the menu.

22. My grandfather always said he wanted to "get out quickly."
    That's why we pushed him down the stairs.

23. What is an orphan doing in an amusement park?
    Find the tallest roller coaster... without a return ticket.

24. Why do blind people hate mazes?
    Because they never find the exit... nor the entrance.

25. My neighbor wanted to "go big."
    That's why we launched it with fireworks.

26. What does a coffin on wheels do?
    It ensures that your last stop will be quick.

27. Why don't the dead tell jokes?
    Because their punchlines always arrive late.

28. My friend wanted a "shocking" funeral.
    That's why his tombstone has LED lights.

29. What's a baby doing in a barrel?

Wait until it turns into a tragic story.

30. Why don't orphans celebrate Father's Day?
    Because they never know if someone will invite them.

31. My grandfather wanted to "rest in peace."
    That's why we buried him with earplugs.

32. What is a corpse doing in a glue factory?
    Makes sure everything stays together forever.

33. Why don't blind people play hide and seek?
    Because they never find anyone.

34. My cousin wanted to "break barriers."
    That's why they buried him with his car.

35. What is a baby doing in the freezer?
    Wait until it turns into a dark ice cream.

36. Why don't dead people wear designer clothes?
    Because nobody sees them where they are.

37. My neighbor wanted to be "unforgettable."
    That's why his funeral was broadcast live.

38. What does a coffin with lights do?
    It shines like a mourning discotheque.

39. Why don't zombies go to the gym?
    Because they are pure bones now.

40. My grandfather always said that he hated clichés.
    That's why his tombstone says: "No jokes here!"

41. What is a baby doing in a safe?
    It shows that what is important does not always have value.

42. Why do orphans hate family photos?
    Because they always go out alone.

43. My cousin wanted to "watch the world burn."
    That's why his cremation was broadcast on a WhatsApp group.

44. What is a corpse doing in a blender?
    Wait until you're part of a smoothie no one will ever try.

45. Why don't dead people wear headphones?
    Because the eternal silence is already music to his ears.

46. My neighbor always said that he loved water.
    That's why we spread it in the nearest river.

47. What does a baby do in a swing without a rope?
    Test gravity one last time.

48. Why don't blind people read love letters?
    Because braille never translates broken feelings.

49. My grandfather asked to be remembered as a hero.
    That's why we put a cape... in his coffin.

50. What is an orphan doing in a bookstore?
    Find a book titled "Families for Beginners."

Leave your review if you want... or not, I don't care.

If you got this far and weren't offended (or maybe you were, but you're still reading because you have more serious problems),**Leave your review**Not that I care much, but it would be nice to know how many of you are still functional after this trip to humorous hell.

Did you laugh?
Did you cry?
Did you consider reporting me?

Any reaction is valid, except staying silent as a corpse... we've done that here many times.

Suggested rating:
Five stars: If you have a black soul, but a strong heart.
Four stars: If you laughed, but you feel like a reserved place in hell awaits you.
Three stars: If you're still wondering what you just read.
Two stars: If you are writing this review from a session with your therapist.
A star: If your sense of humor died before you.

Author's note: The negative reviews will be collected, printed and used as material for my next book. So go ahead and inspire me.

Review or not, I'll still be the Down Clown!

Made in United States
North Haven, CT
25 June 2025